Down and down his eyes slid, making her startlingly conscious that she wasn't wearing a bikini top.

After her swim in the hotel pool before lunch, she had popped up to the room and simply substituted briefs and the tunic for her wet swimwear. And now, because of that shiver—at least she tried convincing herself it was because of the shiver—she felt the betraying tingle of her breasts and realised that their hardened peaks were straining against the soft cotton. Though she couldn't see his eyes, she could feel them on her breasts, and suddenly his mouth quirked, as though he thought himself solely responsible for their shocking betrayal.

Mortified, she turned sharply away, her heart hammering. She was being silly, she thought, shaken. It couldn't be…!

Elizabeth Power was born in Bristol, where she still lives with her husband in a three-hundred-year-old cottage. A keen reader, as a teenager she had already made up her mind to be a novelist, although it wasn't until around thirty that she took up writing seriously. Her love of nature and animals is reflected in a leaning towards vegetarianism. Good food and wine come high on her list of priorities, and what better way to sample these delights than by just having to take another trip to some new exotic resort? Oh, and of course to find a location for the next book...!

THE ITALIAN'S PASSION

BY
ELIZABETH POWER

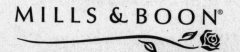

MILLS & BOON®

To Alan—for all your love and support

*First published in Great Britain 2004
Harlequin Mills & Boon Limited,
Eton House, 18-24 Paradise Road, Richmond, Surrey TW9 1SR*

© Elizabeth Power 2004

ISBN 0 263 83726 2

*Set in Times Roman 10½ on 11½ pt.
01-0304-54595*

*Printed and bound in Spain
by Litografía Rosés, S.A., Barcelona*

CHAPTER ONE

HE WAS sitting alone at one of the waterside tables, looking out over the rustic platform that jutted out from the rocks. A man who had produced a ripple of excitement among the female bathers and had had pulses fluttering like the white fringes of the blue sun umbrellas he was now studying with such careless arrogance even before he had stepped out of his dinghy and come ashore.

Now, under the raffia canopy of the beach restaurant, with her sunglasses shielding her eyes from the bright Italian sun, Mel Sheraton's interest was unwillingly drawn to him.

Probably in his mid-thirties, olive-skinned. His strong black hair, combed straight back from a high forehead, reached almost to his shoulders, marking him at once as a man who flouted convention. She couldn't see his eyes because he too was wearing shades, but instinctively she knew that they would miss nothing, that behind them lurked a brain that was hard and shrewd. But it was that profile! Those well-defined cheekbones and that grim mouth and jaw, carved as the rocks to which the white Moorish houses of Positano—partially obscured by the jutting headland— clung dramatically, that filled her with a sudden, disquieting unease.

'OK. He's a dish all right, but you don't have to eat him all at once.' Karen Kingsley's words cut through Mel's absorption, bringing her attention back to the dark-haired young woman sitting opposite her.

'Who?' she parried, with a prudent sideways glance down across the umbrellas to the three young people who were splashing about in the sparkling blue water. Checking, as she had been doing ever since they had finished lunch.

'Oh, come on, Mel. If you hadn't noticed before, he's been looking at you ever since he arrived.'

When, Mel thought tensely, she had done her level best to ignore him. Even so, she had been aware of the power of his presence when, after securing his boat beside the little wooden jetty, he strode across the planking and mounted the steps to a table just metres from their own.

'Don't be silly,' Mel responded, lifting her glass to take a long draught of her mineral water. 'If anyone, he's been looking at you, not me.'

Karen had worked as a model until leaving England two years ago when, newly married, she had emigrated with her artist husband and was now devoting all her time and energy to his small and modern gallery in Rome. But Karen was outstandingly beautiful with her fine, patrician features and expensively bobbed hair, and her shorts and sun top emphasising her long, willowy limbs. Quite a contrast to what Mel considered were her own average features, a body that was unimpressively petite and mutinous auburn hair that went its own way even after the most expert attention.

'You know that's not true. And even if he had been remotely interested—which he isn't—he'd already have noticed the wedding ring and discarded me as unnecessary hassle,' Karen assured her. 'Don't tell me you're immune, not to someone like him, because I shan't believe it, not least because of the way you've made a point of deliberately avoiding looking at him all the time he's been sitting there.'

'Good grief!' Bright tendrils that refused to be constrained in their twisted topknot stirred faintly against Mel's startled face. Was it that obvious?

'Yes,' Karen emphasised in response to her friend's unspoken query, and they both burst out laughing.

Karen was a good friend, Mel thought. They had met

when the model had been promoting the newest sports saloon to come out of Germany in an advertising campaign undertaken by Jonathan Harvey Associates, of which Mel was Sales and Marketing Director. Karen had driven all the way down from Rome to join her here in Positano two days ago. Tomorrow, before the rest of the team arrived, she would be driving back and taking Zoë with her, leaving Mel free to devote her time and effort to the week's conference that she and Jonathan were hosting on the firm's behalf, and Mel couldn't help but feel enormous gratitude to her friend.

Out of the corner of her eye, however, she was aware that the little bubble of merriment just now had produced a subtle glance from behind those dark lenses, even though the man was still engaged in conversation with the waiter.

'I'm not immune,' she stressed more seriously, careful not to look his way. 'But I do have Zoë to think about.' Which was why she had insisted on having a couple of days here alone with the child, ahead of schedule. She didn't even feel guilty any more about putting Jonathan off when he had suggested flying out earlier, joining them today. Just self-contained, she thought resolutely, hardening herself to the caress of the sun on her neck and bare arms, the scent of suntan lotion, sweet herbs and the delicious aroma of barbecued fish. All of them were combining to try and make her drop her guard, forget the lesson she had learnt a long time ago, of how devastating the power of sexual attraction could be. It had cost her everything. Almost.

Instinctively, her eyes returning to the swimmers, Mel saw the twelve-year-old striking out, away from the others.

Any further and she would have to consider calling her back, she decided with an anxiety she knew wasn't entirely justified. After all, Zoë's two teenage companions, who were staying in the hotel, had promised to look after her. Besides, she wasn't that far from the shore, Mel assured herself in an attempt to dispel her unnecessary worries. And

Zoë was a brilliant swimmer. As Mel's sister Kelly had been…

A blade of something, long-buried and acute, sliced unexpectedly through Mel and, for a few moments, from the familiar shape of the girl's head and the trick of light and water that made the dark chestnut hair gleam almost black, Mel had a job convincing herself it was Zoë swimming out there and not Kelly.

The warm breeze passing through her white beach tunic nevertheless made her shiver, and mentally she shook the disturbing images away.

Momentarily off guard, her glance strayed to a pair of broad shoulders beneath the stretch fabric of a white T-shirt, down over bronzed, bare forearms to a fit, lean torso. From where she was sitting she was able to assess that his legs, exposed by dark shorts, were hair-roughened and strong, that his feet were lean and as bronzed as the rest of him in their very masculine flip-flops and without warning an unbidden excitement uncoiled in her stomach.

Then she glanced up, realised with shaming self-consciousness that the waiter had gone and that she was looking straight into those hidden, yet all-seeing, eyes, and for several eternal seconds she couldn't look away.

Caught in the snare of his regard, she felt the pull of a sexual magnetism so great that the animated conversations around her, the chink of glass, the ring of cutlery, seemed not to be part of her world. All that existed was the racing of her blood and that burning gaze she could feel as tangibly as the dappled sunlight through the raffia canopy as it moved over the soft curve of her forehead with its fine dark brows, over her small straight nose and full, slightly parted lips to the long line of her throat, emphasised by the wide slash neckline of her tunic. Down and down his eyes slid, making her startlingly conscious that she wasn't wearing a bikini top. After her swim in the hotel pool before lunch, she had popped up to the room she shared with Zoë and simply substituted briefs and the tunic for her wet swimwear. And now, because of that shiver—at least she tried convincing herself it was because of the shiver—she felt the betraying tingle of her breasts and realised that their hardened peaks were straining against the soft cotton. Though she couldn't see his eyes, she could feel them playing on her breasts, and suddenly his mouth quirked as though he thought himself solely responsible for their shocking betrayal.

Mortified, she turned sharply away, her heart hammering. She was being silly, she thought, shaken. It couldn't be…!

Hardly daring to think, turning her attention seawards in involuntary escape, she froze, colour draining from her flushed face.

'Oh my God!' she whispered, springing to her feet. 'Oh my God!'

'What is it?' Karen asked, but the query was lost beneath the scrape of Mel's chair on the stony surface and the clunk of her tumbler hitting the vinyl tabletop, spilling a pool of melting ice across it as Mel's knee struck one of the legs.

She wasn't even aware of it in her desperate bid for the terrace. Zoë was in trouble, she realised, sick with fear. The two teenagers who had sworn to keep an eye on her weren't even conscious of what was happening. The girl hadn't left the comparative shallows of the rocks and the boy was too preoccupied with his snorkelling to notice anything. But Zoë was trying to swim and, from the frantic splashing of her flailing limbs, was finding it almost impossible even to stay afloat. Mel heard her scream then, the sound ringing ominously across the bay.

'Zoë!' Mel shrieked, heading for the steps to the sundeck, but, quick to assess the situation, the man had reached them first.

He must have leapt to his feet an instant after she had,

Mel realised distractedly, and now he was clearing the wooden steps two at a time.

Fear tearing at her chest, Mel tried to keep up, failing miserably to match his speed as he raced across the platform and on to the jetty. She wasn't even aware of people stirring beneath the umbrellas, or that some of the bathers were already on their feet. Her attention was solely with the man who, poised for a fragmented second, was suddenly plunging into the sea, his body like a dark arrow, before he surfaced, tossing water out of his eyes, arms slicing through the water in a powerful front crawl.

With a mixture of horror and fascination, Mel watched the gap closing between the man and the child, blind and deaf to the onlookers behind her. The teenage boy, suddenly wise to Zoë's screams, had already started to swim out to her. But the man had reached her first and, with a sigh of weakening relief, Mel saw him catch the frightened girl in his capable arms and turn effortlessly with her back towards the shore.

'It's all right. She's all right.' Mel felt a gentle arm go around her shoulders. Karen's, she realised, only conscious then of the sounds of expressed relief coming from behind her on the terrace, of people drifting back to their loungers.

'I shouldn't have let her swim out there on her own. I shouldn't have let her,' Mel repeated, bitterly reproaching herself. 'I should have said "no" and not let her persuade me, not given in.'

'You can't wrap her up in cotton wool,' Karen stated philosophically. 'Of course you should have. She's a stronger swimmer than you are, and besides, she wasn't alone.'

'Wasn't supposed to be,' Mel grimaced, angry. She shouldn't have been stupid enough to trust anyone that young to look after Zoë, she thought, still blaming herself, rushing forward the instant the man lifted the coughing, limping child on to the jetty.

'Zoë.' Her arms going gratefully around the slim, sodden girl, she was oblivious to the man who was now hauling himself on to dry land. Water seeped through her thin tunic and, where the garment had slipped off one shoulder, ran coldly from Zoë's long dripping hair on to Mel's heated skin.

'It's all right, I'm all right,' was the coughed, almost impatient, response from the twelve-year-old. Zoë hated fuss, and Mel knew she wouldn't allow herself to be discouraged for long. 'I just got cramp...' But, as the girl tried to walk, her face twisted in anguish and quickly Mel urged her down on to the decking where, kneeling, she straightened the young limb and gently drew Zoë's left foot upwards towards her shin.

'There's no harm done.' The deep voice drifted down to Mel as she massaged the tightly bunched muscles in the girl's calf. A voice that, despite those Latin looks, uttered only perfect, unaccented English. A voice she would never have forgotten in a million lifetimes. For a few brief moments though, she hadn't realised he was there.

Now she became aware of the long, powerful legs planted firmly beside her, of the water running from him, around his tanned bare feet. He must have kicked off his shoes prior to taking that dive, Mel's brain registered, as it started to get back into gear. 'The leg will probably be sore for a day or two, but your sister's a plucky little lady. It might not be a bad idea to keep a close eye on her over the next few days. These cramps have a habit of recurring.'

Zoë, clearly beginning to feel more comfortable, was grinning at the man's obvious mistake, but right then Mel couldn't share the child's amusement.

Still struggling with self-recrimination, gratitude and now

a deepening dread, Mel placed the young foot gently down
on the decking and rose swiftly to her feet.

'Thank you…' She couldn't go on, rendered speechless
as she tilted her head to meet harshly sculptured features.

'Vann. Vann Capella,' he offered, obviously imagining
that she was waiting for him to introduce himself. Not for
one moment that she was stunned into silence by this unbelievable trick fate seemed to be playing on her.

Vann Capella. He hadn't even needed to tell her his name.
If she had wanted to deny it before, as she looked up into
his face and met the steel-blue eyes—devoid of the sunglasses he had obviously ripped off earlier—then she had to
acknowledge it now. For the best part of fourteen years this
man had haunted her dreams and, if she were honest with
herself, even her waking hours. Never had she thought it
possible their paths would ever cross again. Yet here he was,
like a phoenix rising from the ashes of time to taunt her
with the bitterest of memories.

Mel swallowed, nodded her head, stammered something
like, 'Y—Yes. Well…thank you.' She wasn't even sure herself what she was saying. Whatever it was, it was inadequate
after what he had done, she acknowledged absently, as sen-
tences like *Fancy seeing you here!* and *I wasn't sure it was
you earlier* piled into her mind. But, of course, she hadn't
known him at all, had she? Not really.

Tremblingly, she put a hand to her temple, her face pale
beneath the brightness of her hair. 'I don't know what to
say.'

His smile showed a set of strong white teeth. 'I think
you've said it all,' he returned with impeccable grace.

Briefly, those disturbing eyes flicked over the gold skin
of her bare shoulder. Her tunic, dampened from clutching
Zoë, had to be almost transparent, she realised, where it lay
across the projection of her breasts, leaving their full roundedness apparent to his gaze.

But he hadn't recognised her! Relief made her knees almost buckle.

'Are you all right?' His hand was wet and warm on her bare arm. 'You've had a bit of a shock. Do you want to sit down? Can I get you a drink? A brandy or something?'

Mel shook her head, trying to restore her equilibrium. He was so close she could smell the heady musk of his body, mingling with the fresh salt tang of the sea. His T-shirt and shorts clung wetly to his muscled torso, making her too conscious of the way his skin would glisten beneath them like polished bronze, feel like soft warm leather…

'No!' Shocked by the lethal strength of his sexuality and even more by her awareness of it, Mel pulled sharply away. 'N—no, I'm all right,' she breathed, hoping he would think her confusion stemmed solely from what had happened out there with Zoë.

'You're sure?' His dark eyes were studying her, but with no sign of recognition.

'Yes,' she said, still fighting for her composure. 'Yes, I'm all right. Thank you. And thanks again for what you did for my daughter. We're both very grateful.'

'Your *daughter*?' She followed his surprised glance towards Zoë. The child was still sitting, massaging her cramped muscles, her cornflower blue eyes, shielded by a hand from the sun's glare, looking adoringly up at her rescuer.

'Everyone tells Mum she looks too young to have me.' Her face, like Mel's, was a perfect oval, but with thicker, well-defined brows and a determined mouth that was too strong to be called pretty just yet. 'But I don't mind. I think it's cool.'

'She's a bright kid,' the man commented, mouth tugging down one side.

Under normal circumstances, and with anyone else, Mel would have rolled her eyes and laughed, said something like

Tell me about it!, because Zoë was a precocious child, intelligent, spirited, with a mind of her own. Only these weren't normal circumstances. And this wasn't anyone else. This was Vann Capella. And the man had virtually just saved her daughter's life!

Momentarily reliving the terror that had seized her when she had seen Zoë struggling out there, Mel turned her head away, her eyes stinging with overwhelming emotion. It could have been a terrible tragedy if he hadn't been on hand to prevent it happening. 'It was ironic when she considered it. Not to mention his mistaking Zoë for her sister!

All through lunch he had been sitting there and she hadn't even realised it to begin with. Or had she? She wondered now. Had her subconscious acknowledged him even when she hadn't? Had her physicality recognised his even when her brain refused to, producing that shaming sexual response in her across the tables?

A heated flush stole across her skin. Biting down on her lower lip, she heard him say, 'Are you sure you're all right?'

Swiftly, Mel pulled up her wayward thoughts. 'Of course,' she said, a little too sharply, because, of course, he hadn't recognised her. And why should he? she thought. She'd been no more than a temporary inconvenience in his life. 'Thanks again. Now, I'm afraid we really must go.'

'Oh, Mum! Do we have to?' Zoë groaned, getting up rather tentatively. Clearly she was enjoying the man's company.

He shrugged, turning to Mel with lips compressing as though he had just found an ally.

Strung with tension, without any of her usual patience, Mel said, 'Yes, I'm afraid we must,' almost pulling her daughter with her.

'Perhaps we'll meet again,' he said, but he was smiling down at Zoë. 'And look after that leg.'

'I will.' Zoë beamed, evidently smitten.

A host of conflicting emotions raged through Mel. 'I'm afraid she's leaving for Rome in the morning,' she put in quickly. Then wondered if she had imagined the shadow that seemed to flit across his face.

'Pity,' he expressed, his shrug of regret bringing Mel's reluctant attention to the superb width of his shoulders, to the musculature of his chest beneath the clinging cotton, to the whole disturbing strength of his virility. 'At least stay long enough to tell me your name?'

Every nerve-end was suddenly zinging with a vibrant warning. Holding herself rigid, Mel felt the silence stretch away into timelessness. Behind her, on one of the sun beds, she heard someone cough, heard the familiar clinking sounds of a table being cleared up in the café, caught the shrill cry of a seabird as it homed in, somewhere high above the grey shingle of the beach.

She took a breath and, chancing it, uttered, 'Mel. Mel Sheraton.' Her pulse thumping, she saw his thick dark brows come together, but then his frown was lost in the blaze of his smile.

'Well, Mel Sheraton…' He dipped his head in an ornately gallant gesture. Having made no connection, she thought, relieved. 'I'm pleased to have been of service to you.' Then he was gone, striding down the jetty where, with a swift economy of movement, he scooped up his discarded shoes and glasses and stepped lithely into his boat.

'That was Vann Capella!' A disbelieving voice suddenly reminded her that Karen had been there all the time. 'I was going to tell you that before you raced off after Zoë. Vann Capella,' her friend continued to enthuse. 'And you turned him down flat!'

Against the sound of a high-powered outboard motor bursting into life, Mel took a steadying breath.

'He was only offering me a brandy, Karen. And only because of the state he could see I was in over Zoë.' And

over seeing him again. Over dreading that he would recognise her. Over a lot of things she couldn't even begin to
tell her friend. Or anyone, she thought, watching the dinghy
streak across the open water, leaving a white trail of turbulence behind it. Not now. Not ever.

'He was offering you a lot more than that and you know
it,' Karen said, her tone almost scolding.

'Who is he?' Zoë wanted to know as they moved back
across the terrace. She was still hobbling, though not quite
as badly now.

Something tightened in Mel's chest and the dryness of
her throat made her swallow. She wanted to wake up from
this nightmare. To leave Vann Capella where he belonged.
Firmly entrenched in the past.

'Who *is* he?' Karen echoed, with an incredulous glance
at Zoë, unaware of her friend's turmoil. 'He owns Capella
Enterprises, a conglomerate of international companies that
probably touch every commercial field you could mention.
One of your self-made, well-on-the-way-to-becoming one of
Britain's richest and most eligible millionaire bachelors, if
you please!'

'Anyway, why don't you run along and get an ice cream?'
Mel asked her daughter quickly.

The twelve-year-old shrugged. 'OK. I thought he was
cool, though. For an old guy, that is.'

Karen laughed, though Mel only managed a half-hearted
smile.

'That was cowardly,' her friend remarked when the child
limped off. 'A man shows an interest in you and you won't
even talk about him. Not even to tell your own daughter
who she's just been rescued by. I'm sure she would like to
have known that, before he became a colossus among business tycoons, he was the most dynamic member of the big-
gest thing in modern rock bands. What what it? Eleven,
twelve years ago?'

'It would hardly have meant very much to her,' Mel responded, without bothering to correct the other woman. 'They disbanded before she was even born.'

'And there was some scandal over that, wasn't there? Didn't they have a rather unscrupulous manager or something? Wasn't he responsible for them losing a lot of money so that they ended up virtually penniless? All I know is,' Karen went on without waiting for an answer, 'when they broke up the other members of the band were never heard of again. While Vann came back as the uncrowned king of commerce, having settled all the band's debts single-handedly. Which was rather magnanimous of him. And now...!' She paused, her sigh of admiration saying it all. 'Vann Capella,' she breathed. 'Who would have believed it? Here?'

'Who would?' Mel said with more vitriol than she had intended, and felt the questioning glance Karen sent her way.

'He was right, you know. You do look rather shaken up,' she commented, as Mel, keen to avoid her friend's well-meaning regard, started swiftly up the steps to the restaurant. 'Are you sure you're feeling OK?'

'Perfectly,' Mel sighed. If only Karen would drop the subject!

'I suppose Vann sounded more universal on stage than Giovanni,' to her dismay Mel heard her friend continuing behind her. 'But he isn't wholly Italian, is he? His mother was English, wasn't she?'

'I don't know.' She could have been more helpful, Mel decided, reaching the table they had abandoned in such haste only a short while ago. It seemed like an age to Mel, though, as she stooped to retrieve the canvas bag by the side of her chair. 'I wasn't a fan.'

'Everybody was. Everybody still breathing,' Karen exaggerated, reaching for her own belongings. 'He used to look irresistible, dressed all in black, with that deep, sexy voice. And he didn't use it to sing so much as to whisper low sexy phrases over that bass guitar that used to seem to throb when he played it.' She gave a delicious little shiver. 'It was orgasmic! And yet he hated it, didn't he? The whole music scene. I remember him referring to himself during a business interview some years ago, when the interviewer tried to get him to talk about it, as an Anglo-Italian boy who had found himself in the wrong place at the right time. And that was it. End of subject. He was born to be a business entrepreneur. That's only too obvious. But at the time I could have died when he quit that band.'

Slipping a canvas strap over one shoulder, Mel glanced towards the ice cream bar where Zoë was still deliberating over a bounty of flavours, and grimaced. 'You and fifteen million other teenage girls,' she remarked, with a sharp stab of concealed emotion.

'Probably,' Karen agreed. 'And he still looks great now, only more so if that's humanly possible. I'll bet he doesn't suffer fools. And he probably eats women for breakfast!' The model rolled her eyes, sounding like the love-struck adolescent she had obviously been. 'They don't come much more dynamic-looking than that, do they?'

Mel glanced down at the ground. There was a dampened patch of flagstone from the water she had spilt earlier when she had bumped into the table leg. The glass had been removed, the surface wiped clean by the efficient staff.

'Looks aren't everything,' she said, aware now of the little purple bruise already forming on her knee.

'It's a darn good start.'

'A start for what?' Mel enquired suspiciously, folding her arms as she waited patiently for Zoë.

'Ooh, I don't know…' Karen's lips were pursed. 'Another chance meeting? One stupendous night or two? A raging affair?'

'I thought you were happily married.'

'I am, but I can still admire, can't I? I don't intend trading Simon in for anyone. I was thinking of you.'

Mel laughed, but without any trace of humour. 'Then think again.'

She moved away, looking seaward for a moment. Most of the diners had gone, either down to the beach, to the loungers, or via the dimly lit corridor cut through the mountainside, back to the lift and the funicular railway that would take them all the way back up to the cliff-top hotel. There was only one young couple left, sitting at one of the rear tables near the gaping cavern of the corridor and, without even looking at them, Mel could tell that they were very much in love.

Perhaps feelings like that could last a lifetime for some people, she thought, but, going by her mother's two marriages, she had strong doubts.

'I forgot. You don't go in for one-night stands, do you? Or any kind of commitment, for that matter,' Karen commented, as though wise to her friend's thoughts. 'In fact, in the two or three years I've known you, you've never got involved—I mean, really involved—with anyone. Despite Jonathan's efforts. Not to mention mine and Simon's! You won't give it a chance, Mel—not even with the most innocent of blind dates.' Concern showed in the taller woman's eyes as she studied her friend and said, 'But it obviously hasn't always been like that.'

A bubble of girlish laughter floated towards them from the ice cream bar. Zoë, chuckling over something the middle-aged waiter was saying. Probably she had told him about her cramp and having to be rescued, Mel thought, noticing that he had filled a cone with an extra large helping of ice cream for her. Charmed, Mel decided wryly. Manipulated by that special quality of Zoë's that nearly always guaranteed her daughter her own way.

'That was a long time ago,' Mel said.

'In that case it's time to move on. And turning down multi-millionaires is definitely moving in the wrong direction. You might have screwed up your chances good and proper. He might not be so interested if you bump into him again.'

'Which I'm quite sure I won't,' Mel said meaningfully. 'Anyway, I think he got the impression that both Zoë and I were leaving in the morning. And, even if he hadn't, he really isn't my type.'

'And what is? Someone you'll feel safe with, as you did with Zoë's father? Other men can do that, if you'll only let them get close enough to you. You've got to let your hair down. Live a little, Mel. Have some fun.'

'And you call having an affair with someone like Vann Capella living a little? It would seem more like emotional suicide to me.'

'Because you think you'd be just one in a long line of conquests? You're probably right.' Karen laughed, with sleek dark eyebrows raised. 'But what a way to go!'

'Whatever turns you on,' Mel said dryly, but couldn't control the crack in her voice, the strain she could feel in every tense feature. It was only then that she noticed Karen surveying her curiously.

'It's really personal with you, isn't it?' she whispered. 'You really resent him, don't you?' And, when Mel didn't answer, 'Care to tell me why?'

Mel turned away. The sea was calm now, with no sign of the turbulence left by the dinghy's departure, or of the underlying currents of pain and remorse that were surging through her.

'It's no secret,' she murmured, thinking it a bitter injustice that she should now be burdened with indebtedness to Vann Capella on top of everything else. 'It was in all the papers. He was the man responsible for killing my sister.'

CHAPTER TWO

THE rest of the team were already there when Mel walked into the long, airy conference room on Monday morning. A couple of dozen plushly upholstered chairs had been set out in double rows of four as she had instructed.

She made a swift check of everything else she had requested. Fresh flowers on the table at the front. The screen and projector for her visual presentation. The folders containing the company's welcome pack, the week's agenda, topics to be discussed and reviewed.

'You've certainly worked hard in putting all this together,' Jonathan remarked, coming over to her. He was flipping approvingly through one of the folders. 'Our clients can't possibly fail to be impressed.'

Tall, blond and in his early thirties, Jonathan Harvey was Managing Director of Jonathan Harvey Associates and Mel's immediate boss, although over the past year they had shared a few casual dinners out of office hours.

'I've got a good team,' she acknowledged, glancing over to where Jack Slater and Hannah Merrifield, two of her young sales managers, were busily putting the finishing touches to the venue with two other young executives from Marketing. 'You know me.' She laughed. 'I've just been lazing around.'

'As if!' Jonathan pulled a wry face, tossing the folder down on to the pile he'd taken it from. 'You might look as though you've just stepped out of one of our *Eternal Springtime* ads…' his gaze took in her vibrant, wayward hair, painstakingly secured in a French pleat, her fresh, youthful complexion that required only the minimum of make-up, and the silver-grey suit tailored to her slim, petite figure '…but I know you work harder than anyone.'

Which was encouraging at least, Mel thought, with a mental grimace, glad to be compared with the positive re- sults of a teenage beauty product. Her head, though, felt delicate from two restless nights' sleep, the outcome of hav- ing bumped into Vann Capella down at the beach the other day. Refusing to dwell on that, however, as she had been trying rather unsuccessfully to do ever since, she came back to the present to hear Jonathan saying, 'I see I shall have to watch my own job if you carry on like this.'

Despite everything, mischief lit the green eyes that were emphasised by a smudge of grey shadow. 'You think I might be after it?'

'Who knows?' He sent her a wry glance. 'You're a daunt- ing businesswoman, Mel.' And then, as though needing to remind her, 'Did you enjoy your two or three days playing full-time mother?' he asked.

Dear Jonathan, she thought. She liked and respected him. But even he sometimes had difficulty dealing with her single mother/company director status, perhaps feeling, in some weird way, somehow threatened by it.

'It made a nice change,' she said, because that was what he expected her to say. Not that the job of being a mother ever ended—or the concerns and anxieties of it anyway. But she didn't think he would wholly understand that. Besides, the first clients had started to filter in.

Swiftly, Mel gestured to the rest of her team, who moved over to the door to greet them. Opposite her, Jonathan had taken up his position beside the pretty, fair-haired Hannah who was handing out a welcome pack to each client.

Managing Directors. Chief Executives. Wives and part- ners. These were the higher echelons of their most favoured international clients. Mostly middle-aged or elderly men. Wealthy and successful, if the display of Mercedes, Jaguars and BMWs she could see parked on the scorching asphalt outside was anything to go by. Even as she looked, a black Aston Martin with tinted windows swung in and purred to a halt alongside the others, its subdued colour and low, sleek lines, symbols of understated luxury.

She was talking to a chatty elderly man about the subtleties of advertising when her eyes were suddenly drawn towards the door. Lips parted, shock numbing her, she could only look on in disbelief. Vann Capella!

He was shaking hands with Jonathan, just a few metres from where she was standing, and the blow of seeing him again coupled with his stupendous appearance reduced everything else going on in the room to a blur.

Though it wasn't strictly a formal affair, all the men wore dark suits, white shirts, ties—the uniform of the company man. But it was obvious Vann Capella had not seen fit to conform.

Tie-less, in a light beige suit and open-necked white shirt that contrasted sharply with his tan, his very detachment appeared to mock their stiff formality, so that he seemed the only one appropriately dressed for Positano's stifling heat. The gleaming ebony hair, sleek against his head, was fastened at the nape of his neck today, its severity only seeming to emphasise his hard masculinity. He looked everything he was. Rich and powerful and awesome. Probably one of the youngest men here, Mel calculated, and yet he dominated the room.

Then he looked over and saw her, and the space between them was suddenly detonated with a high and dangerous energy. For fleeting seconds Mel couldn't move, trapped in the snare of a regard that was fiercely intent. But the man who was chattering away beside her suddenly paused, waiting for an answer to a question she hadn't even heard, and quickly Mel pulled herself together.

Bluffing her way through an explanation she hoped made

sense, trying to show an interest she no longer felt, she was suddenly wishing she could be somewhere else. Anywhere but here in this room. With him.

As the clients took their seats, out of the corner of her eye she saw Vann do the same, and her only coherent thought was: what was he doing here? He hadn't arrived when the other clients had throughout the previous afternoon and evening, and his name certainly hadn't been on the guest list. So why had he turned up today?

She didn't know how she managed to get through the morning's agenda, deliver a clear, concise talk on Harvey's new campaigns and its winning promotions, answer questions, and generally appear anything but ruffled. She could only congratulate herself when the whole thing was over and she had managed to sail through it without looking a total fool.

Put it down to professionalism, she thought in wry mockery of herself, as she was reloading her briefcase at the close of the meeting. But all her hard-won competence couldn't stop the leap of her pulse when she glanced up and saw Jonathan leading Vann over to where she was standing, just as she was congratulating Hannah and Jack on the morning's success.

'Vann. I want you to meet my henchman and right hand, Mel Sheraton. Mel.' The MD was beaming like someone who had just landed a prize catch. 'Vann Capella.'

Jonathan, whom Mel had always thought strikingly good-looking, today appeared totally eclipsed by the taller man's overwhelming presence, while behind them Hannah was looking positively awestruck.

Heart thumping, every nerve went on to red alert as good manners forced Mel to accept the hand Vann extended to her.

'How's the water baby?' he queried softly, looking amused.

Not thinking clearly, aware only of that strong male hand clasping hers, for a moment she frowned, then realising, uttered, 'Fine. Fine, thanks.' Her throat felt tight and dry.

'But in Rome?'

Of course. She had told him that much, hadn't she? He didn't seem surprised, however, that she hadn't gone as well. Perhaps, she thought, he had known she was co-host of this conference when he had asked her name down there at the beach the other day, having a distinct advantage over her in that case.

'She's at the age when looking round boutiques is preferable to playing in rock pools,' she murmured unnecessarily, and in a daze heard Jonathan's voice, strung with curiosity.

'Do you two know each other?'

Vann, though, didn't even look his way. Teeth white against his tan, he was smiling down from his superior height and with almost mocking directness was asking, 'Do we, Mel?'

For a moment it was as though there were only the two of them in the room, those soft tones seeming to imply things that were overtly intimate. But the significance of his question rocked her, so that she swallowed, moistened her dry lips. Did he mean simply because of their meeting on the jetty the other day? Or had he recognised her?

In the circumstances, she did the only thing she could. She chose to ignore it and, smilingly, in a voice she prayed she could hold steady, gave Jonathan a résumé of Zoë's rescue.

'I was just quicker off the mark than you were, that's all,' Vann remarked, as though she would have been perfectly capable of his own life-saving abilities. But she could feel him studying the tense contours of her face as though he sensed her unease and was somehow intrigued by it and it was Jonathan who finally broke the awkward little silence.

'Vann's standing in for Austin Heywood, who hasn't been able to get here. Vann took over as Chairman of Heywood last week to try and rescue its Communications Division and, as he's only staying down the coast at his villa, he decided to come himself. He said he hoped we didn't mind.' A purely perfunctory gesture, Mel decided, because she had the strongest suspicion that whatever this mature, stupendous-looking trouble-shooter wanted he would take, regardless of who minded! 'I said we're only too pleased to have such an illustrious client in our midst. That perhaps he could instruct my staff in how to stay ahead of the game. Pass on his expertise and hope that his Midas touch rubs off on Harvey's!'

This produced a burst of laughter from the three of them, though Mel sensed that only Jonathan's was genuine.

So Vann had added yet another string to his remarkable bow! she thought, impressed, yet Jonathan's deference to his prestigious new client irritated her.

'I'm sure anything he could teach us would be worth knowing,' she murmured politely, nonetheless. After all, he was the customer—and a pretty impressive one—and her professionalism wouldn't allow her to be anything but courteous.

'I'll look forward to it,' he said, the smile he flashed her ripe with innuendo. There was, however, something predatory and watchful in the hard glitter of his eyes.

Had something unlocked his memory banks? she wondered, mortified. Did he have any inkling at all as to who she was? He couldn't possibly. Even so, seeing him again had swept the ground from under her. She felt hot and sticky, despite the comfortable coolness of the air-conditioned room. Her head had started to ache, and all she wanted to do was get away.

'Well, it's nice to have met you,' she lied, swallowing to ease the dryness in her throat. 'I'll look forward to talking to you again—' saying it because it was expected of her '—perhaps before the day's through.'

'Sooner than that,' Jonathan chipped in before the other man could say anything. 'Vann's agreed to join us all for lunch.'

All, meaning two of their agency's oldest clients and their wives. Her heart sank.

'How nice,' she responded with a forced smile, determined to keep anyone from seeing through the gloss of her professional veneer. Nevertheless, she could feel those steely eyes upon her and had the distinct feeling that, behind his cool smile, Vann Capella had guessed at the turmoil going on inside her, even if he didn't understand the reason for it.

Lunch was an informal affair, served on the hotel balcony with magnificent views of the mountains and the valley plunging to the sea. Way below them, Positano's quaint houses and colourful hotels huddled precariously on their terraced ledges, a miniature town above the glittering sapphire of the bay.

Business was discussed, and then leisure filled the conversation. The glories of local crafts, the nearby islands of Ischia and Capri. The archaeological phenomenon of neighbouring Pompeii.

'Clever people—these Romans,' John Squire, the eldest of the two client directors remarked. He was a portly, ruddy-faced man in his sixties, who kept slapping his equally rounded wife, Maureen, on the knee.

'Not clever enough to hold on to their empire,' said the other director, a thin, serious-looking man with glasses who was sitting next to Mel.

'That's because they didn't have Vann,' Jonathan said, from Mel's other side. 'If he'd been at the helm two thousand years ago, they would have conquered the universe.'

A chuckle went around the table, murmurs of agreement from the two older men.

'I don't believe my enterprises have yet strayed into the realms of space travel,' Vann commented smoothly, smothering their deference to him with laconic ease.

He had removed his jacket, as everyone else had, and was sitting across the table immediately opposite Mel so that it was difficult to keep her eyes from straying to the broad span of his shoulders, as it was to stop herself from blushing when he sent her a rather covert smile that excited as much as it disturbed.

'It could come,' Jonathan jested. 'There aren't many men who could grab the heart and mind of every young female in the civilized world and then go on to evoke the envy and admiration of every man in commerce and industry today. You were aware that Vann was the driving force behind—' He had been addressing the others but turned towards his prized client, clicking his fingers as if that could produce the name of the long-disbanded fivesome that was eluding him. 'Sorry about this. It was a long time ago...'

'Exactly,' Vann stressed with a smile that only derided that area of his life. 'A mere anomaly on my part. An aberration. Nothing more.'

As she had been, Mel thought with a sudden piercing hurt she hadn't expected to feel. A straying into unwise waters. Best forgotten. Easily dismissed.

She was glad when the appetising-looking and beautifully presented meal was over, because she couldn't actually remember tasting a thing.

'You weren't half as greedy as the rest of us, Mel.' Maureen Squire laughed as they were getting up from the table. 'Resisting all those tempting sweets! Is that how you manage to keep that lovely slim figure?'

This was the cue for everyone's eyes to swivel in Mel's direction, but it was only Vann's she was aware of, moving with silent assessment over her white sleeveless blouse and short straight skirt that seemed suddenly too short beneath his stripping regard.

'Mel could eat for England and never put on a pound.' It was Jonathan, unconsciously drawing greater attention to her sudden loss of appetite. She saw Vann's lips compress, felt his eyes rake disconcertingly over her face, narrowing, darkly perceptive.

'Perhaps you're working her too hard, Harvey. There was certainly no sign of gourmet tendencies today. In fact, England would have lost if it had been counting on her.'

Darn the man, Mel thought, for emphasising the fact, even though she felt that last quip had been a back-handed lob in response to Jonathan's somewhat indelicate remark. But this man had wreaked devastation on her and her family, and the strain of seeing him again had made her head throb. She didn't want to be here, enduring his calculating glances, having him defend her when he couldn't even remember who she was!

'He's right.' Above the sound of the low horn of a fer-ryboat drifting up to them from the distant harbour, Mel realised that Jonathan was still pursuing the subject of her appetite. 'You didn't eat much today. Not sickening for any-thing, are you?' Blond brows drawn together, he was shrug-ging into his jacket. There were some crumbs on one of the dark lapels.

'No, of course not,' Mel said quickly, aware of those hard masculine eyes still watching her. Vann had retrieved his own jacket, but it was hooked casually over one shoulder, and Mel tried not to notice how the crisp shirt pulled tautly across his chest. But complaining of a headache in front of clients was simply not done and so she said, 'It's probably the heat. I never feel much like eating in these tempera-tures.' She just wanted to get away, escape to her room, find some breathing space so that she could begin to decide how to handle this torturous and difficult situation.

Her chance came as the Squires and the other couple departed for an afternoon trip into town in the hotel's courtesy car. Before anyone could protest, Mel quickly excused herself, leaving Vann in the luxurious lobby with her senior colleague.

Her own room was dark and cool. The maid had been in to clean, drawing the curtains and turning on the air-conditioning unit.

Gratefully, Mel crossed to the *en suite* bathroom and changed into her cotton bathrobe. Her head was thumping and, coming back into the bedroom, she poured herself some iced water from the fridge and took a couple of painkillers before pulling back the curtains. Daylight spilled in, causing her to wince from the sudden brightness.

The dark rattan furniture gleamed and the snowy coverlets on the twin beds reflected the cleanliness of the mirror-polished floor-tiles. Now, though, without Zoë's few belongings lying around, the place seemed sterile and empty and, with a sudden crushing loneliness, Mel put down her glass, pushed open the French doors and went out on to the balcony.

All the rooms in the main hotel overlooked the bay. On plunging terraces, countless flights of steps and quiet paths, shaded by the stirring pink heads of oleander and bougainvillaea, gave access on to garden rooms built into the steep rock. In the distance, looking east, lines of orange sun beds decorated the dark shingle of Positano's main beach.

Way above, on the verdant mountainside, a wisp of grey smoke was rising from one of the farmsteads and, from somewhere in the valley, the thin, metallic sound of a church bell rang out the hour.

She had been looking forward to coming here, she thought, feeling the prick of angry tears behind her eyes.

Yet now she was simply dreading the week ahead, and all because of one man.

Vann Capella.

His turning up here had opened up all sorts of wounds and grievances she had thought soothed by time. But they were still there, like skeletons in a dark cupboard, waiting only for the door to be opened to burst out as fully fleshed demons again.

The fact that he didn't recognise her was a blessing in itself, and yet even that small relief had brought its flipside of hurt, anger and bitterness. But why should he have recognised her? she thought, trying to rationalize, trying to justify. She had only met him once, after all, and then she had been just a kid with dark tinted hair cut elfin short, and a boyish figure which in no way represented the more feminine curves she had developed from becoming a mother. Of course he hadn't recognised her. She hadn't immediately recognised him, had she? Not really. Not to begin with. And he had been a celebrity. His face constantly in some magazine or other. While she…she had been just a nobody…

Speared by an emotion she refused even to acknowledge, she pressed her palms against the wells of her eyes, telling herself she was being over-sensitive, that all she was suffering from was a rather large dose of hurt pride.

It was fourteen years ago! her brain screamed at her. *It's gone! Over with! Finished!* But the demons had been let loose, and with them the memories, unchained to torture and shame her.

It was around the time of her eighteenth birthday when the band had come to the city where she had lived with her mother and her sister. Kelly had been obsessed with the band, but particularly with their aloof and brooding lead singer. She had been fifteen years old, a normal, healthy, happy schoolgirl, and she'd eaten, drank, slept and breathed Vann Capella.

Mel remembered how the music coming constantly from Kelly's room had almost driven their mother to distraction. Sharon Ratcliffe, deserted by two husbands, had struggled to bring up her daughters single-handed. But their fathers' defection had produced a close-knit bond between the two girls when Mel, from the age of seven, had taken her four-year-old half-sister under her wing. Together, wrapped in the cocoon of warmth and affection their mother had woven around them, they had learnt a moral self-sufficiency that excluded any male, a strictly female fortress that no man could storm. Mel thought it laughable now how she had imagined her safe, secure world would last for ever. That was until the night of that fateful concert, and then all her illusions had been brutally shattered.

For weeks Kelly had talked about nothing but Vann and the concert her friend had managed to get tickets for. At eighteen, Mel had considered herself above it all. She had been studying at college, working in a café at weekends and holidays, had her own set of interests, friends. As far as she was concerned, raving over rock stars was something schoolgirls did, girls of Kelly's age and, though appreciating the band's music, Mel had thought Vann Capella both arrogant and morose. He had to be, she decided, to appear so mean and magnificent on stage and yet remain so indifferent, almost contemptuous of the mania he was generating among the female population with his image. The other members of the band joked, flaunted obvious good looks and flashed boy-next-door smiles. Vann, always brooding and silent, oozed raw, unadulterated sex.

Which was why Mel had stayed so unaffected by him and had resolved to remain so every time she had caught herself looking up, drawn against her will by the dark persona of the man staring down at her from her sister's bedroom walls. And why she hadn't felt the slightest bit envious when she and her mother had dropped Kelly off at her friend's house on the evening of the concert. Felt very little for that matter because, sitting there in the car, how could she have known she would never see her half-sister again? Because, carried along on a wave of hysteria, Kelly had died screaming over him.

A heart attack, the hospital had said. They had received flowers from the band's manager. Security had been adequate but could have been better, some official judged. People had made the right noises. It was no one's fault. No one, it seemed, was responsible. And, if that wasn't enough to deal with, Vann Capella's remarks, splashed across one of the tabloids only days after she had died, had seemed to tip Mel over a precipice.

It wasn't his problem. That was it, pure and simple.

Anger had warred with grief. She owed it to her sister to let him know exactly what she thought of his cold, insensitive arrogance. He had been oblivious to Kelly's innocent feelings about him, but Mel vowed he would certainly be made aware of hers!

They had been performing at the Albert Hall that night. It was their largest and last UK concert before their big Australasian tour. Mel had known it was her only chance.

She couldn't even remember how she had explained her intended absence to her mother. That she needed to distance herself from a suddenly suffocating household of far-removed cousins and consoling friends? That she needed some time on her own? Whatever, armed only with a map and her determination, she had got into her old, battered Mini and, driven by unreasoning emotion, had headed straight for the south-west.

She knew that she wouldn't have had a cat in hell's chance of getting to see, let alone confront, Vann in London. He and the band would be whisked away before the fans had even blinked. But, by a quirk of fate, a college friend whose brother was involved with the band's promotion had bragged to Mel weeks before about knowing where the band would be staying after their last performance. They were being flown out of London by helicopter to a remote country manor hotel near Bath.

It was well after midnight when she finally saw the sign for the Somerset village and turned the car through the gates, along the tree-lined drive of the exclusive hotel. It was January and the road conditions had been hazardous. Rain had turned to sleet, then snow. The Mini, always temperamental, had broken down during the journey and, after Mel's futile groping about under the bonnet, decided, inexplicably, to start again, so that she reached the Palladian mansion dishevelled and grubby.

Chandelier-lit windows gave her a glimpse of the sheer luxury inside, while outdoor security lighting illuminated several expensive cars parked on a crescent of shingle, and the helicopter-landing pad embedded in the manicured lawn.

Her hollow stomach churned with apprehension and hunger as the Mini rattled into a space between a Porsche and a Rolls Royce. She was exhausted and she hadn't eaten for hours. But justice for Kelly had her scrambling out of the car, carried her feet over the shingle. The sleet stung her face and her thin scoop-necked sweater, light jacket and jeans were inadequate protection from the biting wind.

Her entry to the house was forestalled by a concierge who had heard her car arrive and had come out to investigate. Did she have a booking? Was she a friend of someone staying there? He probably wasn't accustomed to being descended on, Mel remembered thinking later, by a drowned-looking female with an oil-smeared face and hands in the middle of the night.

Somehow, though, she got into the house, demanding to see Vann Capella, her eyes barely registering the eighteenth-century style décor and furnishings, the elegant floral displays, the exquisite Regency furniture.

Eventually, another man appeared. The hotel's manager, Mel realised from his authoritative tone and manner. Who did she want to see? Who had told her the band was staying there? He was afraid he couldn't divulge any information about guests. He asked what her business was and, when she refused to tell him, had suggested politely but firmly that he thought she should leave.

Her resolve to stay right where she was, and until the morning if she had to, finally galvanized him into action.

With cool formality he had asked her to wait and swiftly disappeared, but the tough-looking, cropped-haired man he returned with wasn't half as polite.

Who the hell did she think she was coming there demanding to see anyone from the band? How had she got hold of the information anyway? The pressure of his fingers bruised her arm as he hustled her towards the door. If she didn't go right there and then, he said, he'd call the police. It was only later that she had discovered he was Bern Clayton, the band's manager. For him, evicting just another pestering teenage fan was par for the course.

Angrily, Mel told him who she was, asserting that Vann *would* see her. She pulled forcibly out of the man's grasp.

'I'm Kelly Ratcliffe's sister,' she threw at him bitterly, as if that would make a difference, believing it with all her naïve confidence of what was right and wrong.

He said he was sorry about her sister, but if she wanted to make a case out of it then she'd better get in touch with her solicitor. It wouldn't do any good, he advised her, taking it out on Vann. So why didn't she be a sensible girl and run on home?

Close to spent, Mel clung to the little fight left in her.

'I'll wait,' she said, folding her arms to emphasise her intention.

'Have it your own way.' The man took his phone out of his pocket, began dialling the police.

And then from behind him came another voice, deep and resolute, brooking no resistance. 'I'll see her.'

It was the first time Mel had seen Vann Capella in the flesh. Neither his photographs, nor his television appearances, could capture the sheer presence of the self-assured youth who had become every girl's dark fantasy, or that powerful sexual aura he wore like a blazing shield.

Framed by the pillared doorway to one of the magnificent staterooms, he was taller than Mel had expected, that air of cold arrogance more daunting, that familiar detachment one of almost hostile rebellion. He was wearing a black vest top and trousers, with an unbuttoned denim shirt slung loosely over the top. He looked as though he had just dragged himself out of the shower, Mel thought, because the thick black hair, worn shorter then, was still damp. Not so much handsome as formidably attractive, even at twenty-two there was a physical force and strength behind that wide brow and proud nose, in the brooding mouth and uncompromising jaw line that set him apart as a born leader, making him a match for his elders and superiors alike.

'You!' Mel breathed at the same time as Bern Clayton swung round, swearing viciously.

'For heaven's sake, Vann!' he snarled. 'Are you mad?'

'Probably.' His whole manner defied the older man as he moved with lithe youthfulness away from the doorjamb. 'What is it to you, anyway?'

Mel sensed that there wasn't too much accord between Bern Clayton and probably his most money-spinning, if not his most manageable, client. But the manager wasn't giving up that easily.

'For goodness' sake! Think of the trouble you could get yourself into,' Mel heard him urge imperatively.

'Don't worry, Clayton. I'm sure you can sort it out for me,' Vann drawled in what was to Mel a dry, uncaring tone so that, driven by hurt anger and injustice, her temper finally snapped.

'And why not?' Somehow she found the strength to raise her voice to him. 'It isn't your problem, is it?' And then, triggered by something beyond her control, all restraint was suddenly deserting her.

Her behaviour was totally out of character, and afterwards would shame her as much as it surprised the two men. Afterwards, too, she would have time to consider how she must have appeared to Vann: a bedraggled waif flying at him like some manic, mindless shrew. At the time, however, she was scarcely even aware of the manager's arm shooting out to stop her, or of Vann thrusting it aside to take the full brunt of her anger.

She knew only the texture of his skin as her nails dragged down the hard bone of his cheeks and shadowed jaw, met the resisting strength of muscle beneath rough denim.

He caught her arms then, which left her clawing at thin air, and suddenly everything became too much. The room started to spin. Weak with exhaustion and lack of nourishment, she felt her legs buckle under her and, with a small sob, collapsed against his hard leanness like a limp doll.

CHAPTER THREE

WHEN the dizziness receded, and her brain started to function again, she was sitting, with her head bowed, on the silky brocade of a chaise longue. Beneath her feet was a thick carpet, softly illuminated by subdued lighting, and on which, planted firmly apart, was a pair of dark, very masculine shoes.

'Feeling better now?'

The deep, concerned voice brought Mel's head up, her gaze lifting from that confident stance to take in the whole length of Vann Capella's hard, rangy body.

Long legs, narrow hips and waist. Black singlet stretched tautly across a smooth, tanned chest. He had discarded the loose shirt, which he must have simply thrown on earlier, exposing muscular arms and shoulders and a lot of swarthy flesh. His drying hair was curling slightly now against his neck, as dark and untamed as a gypsy's. But it was those terrifyingly attractive features—the brilliance of his steely-blue eyes beneath their thickly arched brows and heavy lashes—that for a few moments held Mel in thrall, commanding as much as they were compelling. And he had asked her if she felt better.

Dry-mouthed, she nodded. She hadn't expected him to be so menacingly beautiful. Behind him, in pride of place among the elegant eighteenth-century style furnishings, was an enormous four-poster bed.

'Sorry,' he apologised, as she shot him a swift, censuring look. 'All the public rooms were occupied and in view of the...nature of your visit *and* your rather...delicate state...I thought you'd want some privacy,' he concluded.

Mel put a hand to her temple, trying to take things in. The elaborate room. The doorway giving her a glimpse of an equally elaborate bathroom. So this was his suite.

'I passed out?' She met his eyes full on now. They were clear and cold and penetrating.

'In some style,' he said, grimacing, and she noticed how cruel his mouth was. Cruel and hard and sensual.

The memory of her behaviour in the lobby, however, returned with shaming clarity, making her blush to think of it. 'And you carried me here?'

'As I said, I thought you'd want some privacy. But my motives weren't entirely unselfish. If I was going to be laid into,' he acknowledged, slipping his hands into his pockets, 'I didn't particularly relish the idea of an audience. Even if some members of the media think I shouldn't even sneeze without it making front page news.'

He sounded coldly cynical and not the least bit Italian. Vaguely, Mel remembered Kelly telling her that he had spent most of his life in England.

'All right. I shouldn't have attacked you,' she admitted, stopping short of a full apology. After all, he didn't deserve one, did he? 'But you asked for it.' Just thinking about what he had told the press started her anger brewing again. 'You're nothing but a callous, arrogant bastard! How do you think we felt reading what you said about Kelly? Dismissing her like that? And then going ahead with your tour like she was nobody? *Nothing!*' She was shouting now, but she couldn't help herself, unleashing her pain and anger with every syllable she threw at him. 'Didn't you care that she might just have a family who might be going through hell over what had happened? How would you have felt if the same—'

'Terrible.'

'—thing had…' Her sentence drifted away, that one word stunning her into silence. Open-mouthed, she stared up at him, her eyes dark hollows in the small pale oval of her face.

'Terrible,' he reiterated, though that harshly sculpted face was hard to read.

'So why did you say it?' she whispered.

Beneath his incredibly thick lashes, Vann's eyes were unfathomable, yet for a moment, held by the intensity of their penetrating regard, Mel's bones seemed to liquefy, but from something other than mere fatigue this time.

'I didn't.'

'What do you mean, you didn't?' Accusation stole into her voice again. 'I read it. So did the whole of Britain probably!'

'I'm sure they did.' A muscle pulled beside that cruel mouth. 'But one thing you learn in this business is never to put all your faith in everything you read. I was misquoted,' he expounded bluntly. 'What I did say was that Kelly had a problem. A heart defect.' It was something that hadn't been known until after she had died. 'That, tragic though it was, the band couldn't shoulder responsibility for what had happened. That it wasn't anybody's fault. It makes better reading to transcribe it as though I didn't care. Far more sensational. Sells more newspapers, too. But I didn't say it. Nor would I. I'm not entirely... What was it you called me? A callous, arrogant bastard?' A black eyebrow lifted in an almost self-denigrating manner. 'And I had to go ahead with the tour. Like it or not, I'm under contract. I've got commitments—responsibilities to other people. I'm sorry it happened,' he said, removing his hands from his pockets. 'And I appreciate how you feel. I'd probably feel the same way— maybe worse—if the situation were reversed. But it really wasn't anyone's fault.'

Feeling the weight of grief pressing on her chest, Mel couldn't answer. She looked down at her hands, studying them as though she hadn't seen them before. They were grubby from tending to the car.

It wasn't anybody's fault, he had said. All the time she had been concentrating her efforts on blaming Vann, confronting him, yet hearing his side of the story shook her convictions to the core. There seemed to be more than a ring of truth to it, a forthrightness behind that dark, enigmatic persóna that came dangerously close to making her believe everything he said. But someone had to take responsibility! It wasn't enough, his trying to tell her that nobody was to blame!

'It should never have happened! It should never have been *allowed* to happen!' The tears she had held bravely back over the past few days threatening to overwhelm her, she jumped up, anger the only thing left holding her together as she vented her outrage and misery on bands, the Establishment, Vann for being who he was, lashing out in one last desperate tirade to try and ease the unbelievable pain inside her. 'You shouldn't be allowed to do what you do when you know what it does to girls like Kelly! It's all for the fame—the adulation! She was only fifteen years old, for God's sake! Just a kid! Just a sweet, innocent kid and you killed her! You all killed her!' Tears were gushing from her now. Helpless in her grief, she sank to the carpet, her clawed hands turning into fists, thrashing out at the chaise longue, at the world, only hurting herself as her hand struck something hard and wooden.

'For Christ's sake…!' Swiftly he came down on his knees, catching her hard against him, holding her fast so that she couldn't do herself any more harm, imprisoning her arms with the determined power of his. 'It's all right! It's all right! Come on! Come on! It's all right!'

She was crying hysterically, her sobs only muffled by the warm, cushioning strength of his shoulder.

Quickly he carried her over to the bed, sat down with her

between the draped curtains, still clutching her tightly to
him, whispering soothing words, rocking her as one would
rock a baby.

'Hush. Hush. It's all right. It's going to be all right.'

He rocked her until her racking sobs began to subside.

Gradually, as she calmed down, she became acutely conscious of those strong bare arms around her, of that smooth
velvet chest beneath his vest and his intoxicating scent.

'Are you all right?' he asked as she stirred against him.

She nodded, pulling away from him, sitting up. 'I feel a
mess,' she sniffed, raking her fingers through her hair. She
grimaced as she looked down at her other hand.

'If you think they're bad…' He didn't have to finish. A
wry glance at her face said it all. He gave a jerk of his chin
towards the *en suite* bathroom, moving swiftly to assist her
as she shrugged out of her jacket.

'Can you manage?'

'Yes.'

In the luxurious bathroom she splashed soapy water on
her mascara-stained cheeks, patting them dry with a fluffy
towel that smelt of his shower gel. Hopelessly then she tried
to tug her hair into some sort of shape.

Her face in the glass looked drawn and pale, and her
eyelids were red and puffy. Behind her, reflected in the mirror, beads of water still clung to the glass and tiles of the
shower cubicle. From where he had been cleaning up before
he'd come downstairs, she remembered, wondering if he
had come down at once, or if he had given it some consideration.

Her tired thoughts running riot, she imagined him leaping
under the welcome jets as soon as he'd stepped off the helicopter, drenched in perspiration after his performance. He
would have looked ungovernable, his clothes clinging to
him, would have been exuding a raw, animal aroma…

'Are you OK in there?' His deep voice brought her out of her disconcerting reverie.

She moved back into the bedroom, so tired she could scarcely walk straight. Vann was reaching for his shirt on the bed, tossing it down on to the chaise. He glanced towards her as she dropped down on to the white coverlet.

'I'd better go,' she said, reaching exhaustedly for her jacket.

As she made to get up, however, a determined hand was on her shoulder, pressing her gently back down.

'You're not going anywhere,' he stated firmly. 'You're not in a fit state to stand, let alone drive! I presume you drove here?'

Mel uttered a small sound of confirmation. 'I can't stay here,' she argued feebly. She had very little cash with her and her credit limit certainly didn't extend to the prices charged in a hotel of that calibre.

'You can and you will,' Vann asserted in a tone that defied argument and, with one fluid movement, was lifting her legs up, swivelling her round fully on to the bed. 'I'm taking responsibility for you tonight, so you can protest all you like. You're staying.'

'Then…where will you sleep?' she asked hesitantly.

His glance followed hers to the chaise.

'Well, I'm sure that would be the gallant thing to do,' he accepted wryly. 'But I'm far too exhausted for that. Oh, don't worry,' he added, seeing the startled look that darkened her eyes. 'I've just done the gig of my life. Given every ounce of mental and physical energy in the process. I've got none left for anything save getting a good night's rest.'

Already he was removing her sneakers, black hair falling loosely across his brow.

'When did you last eat?'

'I don't know.'

'Then I'll ring down for something.'

'I'm not hungry.'

'Maybe not, but you've got to eat.'

He reached down for the phone on the bedside cabinet, started tapping out some digits. As if he was really concerned about her, she thought, listening to him ordering room service. As if he cared…

'Why didn't you just throw me out?' she asked wretchedly as he came off the phone.

'As Bern Clayton would have done?' And, when she frowned, 'Our manager,' he went on to enlighten her. 'The guy you met downstairs. Contrary to what you might have thought…' He paused, black brows drawing together. 'I'm sorry,' he said. 'I don't even know your name?'

Those clear, penetrating eyes seemed to take her breath away. But she answered croakily, 'It's Lissa.' She was going through the fad of hating her name, and used the derivative she was currently demanding her friends and family call her.

'Well…Lissa…' On his lips it sounded rich and warm, unbelievably sensual. 'As I said, I'm not totally heartless.' He was walking away from her, towards the bathroom, the easy grace of his movements capturing her gaze without her even being aware of it so that she was totally unsettled when he suddenly turned, caught her watching him. 'And you're wrong. It isn't all gold and glory in this business. It's cutthroat and exploitative. And sometimes the superficiality of it all makes me sick!'

The vehemence of his words surprised her. She had thought he wallowed in his fame. Yet now…

She was still trying to come to terms with her new concept of someone she was beginning to realise she had misjudged when the food arrived.

'Just one more spoonful,' he urged ten minutes later when she was forcing herself to swallow the thick home-made vegetable soup he had ordered with a basket of warm crusty rolls. He was sitting on the edge of the bed where she sat, propped up against several plump pillows.

'I can't.' Tiredly she let her spoon drop back into the half-emptied bowl.

He leaned forward to inspect it. 'Well, I suppose you've eaten enough,' he conceded, taking the bowl from her, the movement causing a waft of his pleasant, elusive scent to impinge on her nostrils. He obviously hadn't shaved since before his performance, as all he had probably been planning to do after his shower was go to bed, and the darkening shadow around his jaw only added to that thoroughly untamed image. Just above, on one of his cheeks, were a couple of small red marks.

Where her nails had caught him, Mel realised, horrified.

'I'm sorry I scratched you,' she said, contrite.

His thick lashes came down in silent acknowledgement of her apology, black against the dark olive of his skin. Suddenly, though, those amazing eyes lifted, clashed unexpectedly with hers, making her pulse seem to stop and then double its rhythm.

'Did you tell your parents you were coming here?'

Mel swallowed. He was so unbelievably…perfect. 'No,' she answered. 'Anyway, I'm eighteen. I can do as I like.'

'So grown up.' His smile was the most disarming thing about him, she decided at that moment, because he didn't do it very often, and with a shocking realisation found herself wondering, in spite of everything, what that cruel mouth would feel like against hers. More soberly then, he said, 'None of us can do as we like. We all have some responsibility to someone or something.'

As he had said he had to others involved in the tour?

She wondered how she had ever thought him selfish and arrogant. Well, just a little bit arrogant maybe, but not cold or callous as she had thrown at him earlier. He was caring. Considerate. Tender, even…

Just thinking about how tender he might be in a totally different situation caused a funny little feeling in her stomach. Her heart was beating ridiculously fast as he stood up.

'Won't anyone be worried about you?' His eyes were faintly puzzled. 'Shouldn't you call them?'

She shook her head. 'I needed to be alone. To get away. Anyway, it isn't my parents. It's just Mum and—'

She brought herself up quickly. She wouldn't cry again. She wouldn't! Swiftly, she pressed her lids against her burning eyes.

'Get some rest,' he murmured softly, and she felt his hand, strong yet understanding, on her shoulder. 'You'll have more strength to deal with it after a good night's sleep.'

She was crying in her dreams. Running weightlessly through a flat, empty landscape, calling out because she had lost something precious, frantically searching every identical blade of grass. There was only one massive tree in a vast endless field and, reaching it, gratefully she sank back against it, grasping the sturdy branch that somehow lay across her chest. The sun must have been playing on its trunk and branches because she could feel its warmth against her, and she felt comforted, secure and safe.

She groaned in her sleep, a low, pitiful moan.

'It's only a dream.' The deep voice was filtering down through the leaves of the tree. 'It's only a dream. It's all right. You're dreaming. That's all.'

Her eyes fluttering open, for a moment, lying there in the darkness, Mel couldn't remember where she was. Then it all came flooding back. Kelly. The desperate drive. Meeting Vann...

As consciousness returned with all its cruel reminders, she uttered another involuntary groan, suddenly aware that the warmth she could feel wasn't the sun but a shadowy, naked torso leaning over her, and the branch lying across her wasn't a branch at all, but a strong masculine forearm gently shaking her.

'Are you all right?' Vann asked.

She wasn't, but she nodded, fully awake now. A sliver of cold moonlight peeping through a chink in the heavy curtains lent a satiny sheen to his skin. The arm that had roused her now lay along the length of his body, which was half-covered by the bedclothes, and Mel wondered, with a sudden dryness in her throat, if he had stripped off completely before coming to bed.

He must, however, have pulled the covers up around her after she had fallen asleep, because she was too warm in her sweater and jeans. Meeting some resistance as she tried to throw them back, she realised that it was Vann's body weight that was stopping them, that he himself was only covered by the bedspread.

Either he liked to sleep in the cool or had wanted to give her extra privacy, she decided, too haunted by her thoughts to feel grateful to him at that moment.

'She was all I had besides Mum,' she whispered, staring face up into the darkness. 'I keep thinking that if I'd been there—gone to that concert with her—it might not have happened. She wanted me to at first, and I wouldn't.'

'Don't,' he said.

'Don't what?'

'Don't torture yourself like that. You couldn't have prevented what happened.'

'But I keep thinking that if I'd given in to her wishes for once—hadn't been so selfish—'

'It probably wouldn't have made the slightest bit of difference,' he said. 'She did what she wanted to do—so did you—and if you could have the time over again you'd do exactly the same thing. It's only natural, what you're feeling. It's just one of the recognised phases of grief which we all have to go through when we lose someone.'

She turned to look up at him, her face a pale, perplexed oval in the moonlight. 'What phases?'

'Disbelief. Anger. Self-reproach. Killing while it lasts. But you learn to judge yourself a little less harshly in time.'

He sounded as though he'd had first-hand experience. As though he knew. What was it Kelly had said? Mel reflected, wanting to remember, rifling through her memory banks and her sister's interminable ravings about him. That his father had died from…What was it? A heart attack? And his mother from an overdose of something less than a year later when he was, what, only fourteen?

Mentally she winced from the depth of anguish he must have suffered, unable to dismiss it now as lightly as when Kelly had tried to stir her reluctant sympathies towards him.

'It just hurts,' she murmured and, on a shuddering little breath, '*So* much.'

The arm that had been resting in an arc above her head now slipped around her shoulders, comforting, like the tree in her dream, sure and strong and protective.

'The deeper you love the more it's going to hurt.'

'I wish I hadn't,' she said poignantly. 'I wish I didn't love anyone.'

He gave a soft chortle through the darkness. 'You don't mean that,' he assured her equally softly. 'It can only be good to have loved someone—have someone love you— that much. Not everyone's that lucky.'

Something in his voice made her wonder if he was referring to himself. She looked up at him questioningly, but his face was a series of dark angles and planes, made harder by the shadows.

'I suppose not,' she breathed, feeling an insidious tension stealing through her, a heat that sprang from more than just the cocooning warmth of the magnificent four-poster bed.

There was a vulnerability to his mouth as he gazed down on the paleness of her throat and the delicate collar-bones exposed by the wide slash-neck of her sweater and for a moment she wanted to reach up, touch the hard line of his jaw. Then his eyes lifted, locked with hers, and she felt she was drowning in two lonely pools.

'Tomorrow...' he said huskily, reaching across to trace a finger down the soft curve of her cheek '...you'd better give me your telephone number.'

'My...telephone number?' Trembling from his touch, she turned her face into his palm, felt its calloused warmth against the corner of her mouth. Breathing shallowly, unconsciously she tilted her chin, moulding her skull to the curve of that arm that felt so warm and comforting, felt so right...

But suddenly he was rolling away from her.

'I'd better get up,' he said.

It was as though a lifeline had been suddenly snatched away from her. She was back in that empty landscape. Lost. Desolate. Cold.

'Don't go!'

He had already tossed back the bedspread, but her small plea stalled him. Wearing nothing but a pair of dark briefs, he was looking at her over his shoulder, his profile harshly outlined.

'You don't know what you're saying,' he reprimanded softly.

Mel's throat contracted. 'Yes, I do.' As she had sat up her sweater had slipped off one shoulder, and her moon-bathed flesh was smooth and pale. 'I don't want to be alone.' In the silvered light she looked young and vulnerable, both of which contributed to a soft sensuality she wasn't even aware of. 'Please hold me,' she whispered.

The gentle curve of her face complemented the hard-hewn angles of his. Where her softness yielded, Vann's austerity seemed unrelenting and rigid. For a few eternal seconds his lashes lay darkly against the wells of his eyes. The lower line of his mouth was drawn tautly in check, and his body seemed caught in the grip of some tight constraint. But then his shoulders relaxed and, as though he had just lost a battle with himself, he released a long sigh and opened his arms to her.

'Come here,' he breathed, and even that sounded like a command.

Tentatively, Mel shifted her position, easing into his embrace. Beneath her cheek the contours of his chest felt like warm, cushioned velvet and she could hear the hard, heavy rhythm of his heart.

'You test a man's strength. You know that, don't you?' he said, again in that slightly scolding tone, that smooth chest expanding beneath her palm.

'Do I?' It was an innocent response, one Mel could hardly voice for the sensations ripping through her.

She had had boyfriends in her young life. Teenage boys whose semi-nakedness she had snuggled up to during innocuous kisses on a beach. A young male body wasn't entirely a mystery to her. But no one had ever affected her as Vann was affecting her now. Her body ached for even closer contact with his. Never, she realised with sudden startling intensity, had she needed this closeness with another human being so much.

His chin brushed her hair and she lifted her head, seeking more than the clasp of those strong arms around her, seeking his comfort, his strength, and with them total oblivion from her misery.

Growing bolder from her need, she did as she was aching to do and let her fingers stray to the rough stubble of his jaw, tracing the path where her nails had tried so viciously to wound. The texture of his skin sent something like a volt of electricity zinging through her. Unconsciously, his name tumbled from her parted lips.

For a second he dipped his head, his mouth a hair's

breadth from hers. But then strong fingers locked around her wrist, halting her caresses.

'You don't want to do this,' he said hoarsely.

'Do what?' she whispered, barely reasoning, knowing only that she wanted to give of herself, to take away the pain, the loneliness or whatever it was she sensed behind that cool detachment and, in doing so, find merciful obliteration in his hard strength.

'You know very well.'

'Yes.'

'And you don't care?'

'I don't want to care.'

'Because you're unhappy and overwrought.'

She knew he was right, but she couldn't accept it because his mouth was so close to hers that she could feel the feather-light touch of his breath fanning her skin, and because the intensity of his gaze seemed to be mesmerizing her so that all she could do was close her eyes against it.

'Please,' she uttered, her emotions laid bare on that one small, tremulous note.

She felt the tension in his body, heard the way his breath seemed to catch in his lungs. Then his mouth was covering hers, and with such intense fulfilment of her longing that she sobbed against his lips, glorying in the strength of the arms that were suddenly locking her to him, not in comfort now but in a hard, sensual demand.

Unused as she was to such raw, masculine passion, Mel met it nevertheless with a feverish urgency of her own. Her fingers revelled in the thickness of his hair, in the smooth rippling satin of his shoulders and the hard musculature of his back.

His mouth was devouring her with its hungry insistence, burning kisses along her cheek and jaw, over her willing mouth, moving with electrifying skill down the sensitised length of her throat. His hand had slipped under her top just above the low waistband of her jeans, its shocking warmth against her bare midriff causing her to suck in her breath.

With heart-stopping anticipation she felt his fingers shape the curve of her hip. She jerked against him with a small guttural cry as shock waves of pure pleasure cascaded through her lower body.

'Easy now. Easy,' he murmured against the slope of her bare shoulder, yet he sounded flattered by her sensitivity to his touch.

Her breasts ached beneath the confining fetters of her clothes and she strained against his naked warmth, the action bringing her into sudden contact with the extent of his own arousal.

'Yes,' he agreed breathlessly, his mouth burning over her throat, and he made short work of removing her top and the white balcony bra, exposing her small breasts and the curvature of her waist and hips to his hot gaze.

She wondered what he thought of her, how she compared with all the other girls he might have had his pick of and undressed like this. And then she remembered that he hadn't picked her or intended to sleep with her. But he must like her a little to have been so gentle with her when they'd met, she considered, because no one had ever shown such tenderness towards her before. She only wished she was more experienced and didn't suddenly feel so unsure of herself, especially when he moved to remove her jeans and her skimpy briefs, then remove his own, and she saw him in all his masculine glory. He was so utterly perfect, proud and confident in his nakedness.

But then, as if reading her thoughts, he murmured, 'You're beautiful,' before dipping his head to taste the sweet bud of one burgeoning breast.

Everything seemed to spiral in a dizzy haze of sensation. The touch of his hands on her body, his hard length nudging at her softness, that exquisitely suckling mouth. She could hear the sleet outside, beating against the windows, the harshness of the night emphasising the warmth and sensuality of the world within. The sumptuous draping curtains above them were like silent witnesses to their passion, absorbing her cries of pleasure and Vann's deeper groans of need. And all at once she was aware that she wasn't shy any more, but confident of her own sexuality, glorying in her naked femininity laid out before him on the sensuous bed.

'I haven't any protection,' Vann said, in a voice thickened by desire. 'I should have done something about it before. But I can get some.'

An icy chill swept across her body as he started to move away. Desperately she clutched at his arm. 'It's all right. It doesn't matter.'

He stopped, frowning down at her. 'You're on the Pill?'

She didn't answer. How could she, when the truth meant that he would leave her? And he couldn't leave her. Not now! Not for a minute!

In response she brought her arms above her head in a gesture of total surrender but with a rather uncertain smile, nervous suddenly of the unknown.

He inhaled sharply and came down to her again, taking her silence as a 'yes'. But he didn't enter her at once, making certain she was ready, kissing the places where his lips and hands had explored, while she sobbed and writhed beneath him, her untutored body hungering for the unleashed power of his.

When it came, she let out a shuddering gasp as anticipation dissolved into mindless sensation. There was no pain, just an abandoned, exquisite ecstasy as he pushed into her.

She lifted her hips, her body yielding easily to accommodate his, and then he was filling her, wholly and completely, taking her with him into eternal, timeless space.

Some time afterwards, snuggled up to him with her head

on his chest, she murmured, 'You understand, don't you? What it feels like?'

'Yes.' He didn't need to ask. He knew she was referring to his parents.

'You must have been devastated.'

'Yes.'

'What happened?'

He stirred slightly, his body tensing as though he were steeling himself against remembering. 'You wouldn't want to know.'

'Tell me,' she pressed softly, raising herself up to touch her tongue to the warm velvet of his shoulder. It tasted slightly salty.

'A mutual exchange of trust?' Cynicism filtered through the soft tones. 'Is that what intimacy does? Drags out your darkest secrets?' And before she could respond, feeling somehow reprimanded, as though she had touched on something far too personal, he was saying, 'I thought it was common knowledge my father drank himself to death and my mother killed herself.'

The bluntness of his statement made her flinch. 'Why?' she whispered, sensing the anguish behind those bitter words. 'How could she leave you like that?'

'I guess she just missed my father.' His breath seemed to tremble through his lungs. 'God knows why! They were never happy. Between her wanting England and his wanting Italy, sometimes they spent months at a time apart.'

'What happened to you?' She laid her head on his chest again, felt its warmth against her cheek, his arm flex around her. 'Who did you live with?'

He made a cynical sound down his nostrils. 'Whoever won.'

'Won?'

'Oh yes, they fought tooth and nail over that little issue. Do you know what it's like,' he breathed, 'feeling as though

you're just a weapon for one parent to hurt the other one?'
His hand was moving absently along her arm, stroking, idly
caressing. 'I suppose they could have divorced. But ethics
and a strict moral upbringing decreed otherwise, in spite of
my father's drinking, his violence, although my mother
didn't help herself on that score. She only provoked him,
which made matters worse. But I came along too soon in
their marriage and they never stopped reminding me of that
fact. Sometimes I felt that they wouldn't have been in the
mess they were in at all if it hadn't been for me. Most of
the time I felt like a whipping boy for a double dose of
resentment. Then, after they died, all I felt was guilt. Sheer,
crucifying guilt!'

'I'm sorry,' she breathed, shocked by what he had told
her, her heart swelling with tenderness and compassion for
him. The image he portrayed on stage wasn't an image at
all, but the real man, she thought. The detached, self-
sufficient, lonely Vann. Inside this wild-looking youth there
had been pain as great, if not greater than hers, she realised,
even if it had been somewhat assuaged by time. And at least
she had known love, security...

'I'm sorry,' she whispered again, her hand caressing the
warm plane of his chest, and didn't need to ask him anything else. At some time or another she had read about the
rest. The foster homes. The jobs he had had. Hard, unde-
sirable jobs, demanding all his time and strength—until one
night in a bar he'd picked up the guitar abandoned by someone who had just walked out of the band...

But she didn't want to think about that because, without
her realising it, his hands had turned exquisitely arousing.
Neither had she realised how hers were affecting him until
she heard him groan. But suddenly he was rolling her over,
taking control again, and with a small moan of acquiescence
she was meeting his insistent passion, welcoming it with a

need as desperate as his until she was lost again in an all-consuming conflagration of the senses.

An unfamiliar whirring sound woke her. Grey morning light filtered through the chink in the curtains, showing Vann's side of the bed to be empty. The dent in his pillow made her smile as she remembered their abandoned lovemaking.

Scrambling naked out of bed, she reached the window and peered through the curtains just in time to see the helicopter lift up and away into a sky leaden with snow.

A knocking on the door made her swing round. Vann!

With her heart leaping, she whisked the thick curtain around her. 'Yes?' she called out, breathless with anticipation.

But it was Bern Clayton who strode in, big and brazen in a grey track suit, stopping dead when he saw her shielding her nakedness in the room's expensive furnishings.

'Where's Vann?' she enquired, looking past him, as though expecting his dynamic young client to come striding in after him.

'Gone. What did you expect?' he told her ruthlessly. 'He's got a TV interview and then a plane to catch. If you wanted to say goodbye to him, I'm afraid you're a little too late.' Then, seeing her wounded eyes, he said with a little more compassion, 'Perhaps he didn't want to wake you. He told me to see that you had a good breakfast and everything you needed to get home.'

Home. And then she remembered that he had asked for her telephone number. Probably because he knew he would be making an early start.

'He said he'd contact me, but he doesn't know where to find me,' she realised, horrified. She would need to rectify that. 'He asked me to leave my number. If I write it down before I leave, will you see that he gets it? He asked me specifically, you see.'

The man's gaze went from her shielded nudity to the incriminating chaos of the bed. 'Was that before? Or after?' he enquired brutally.

Mel moistened her lips. What was he suggesting? She saw him shaking his head, saw the censuring pity in his eyes and felt a gnawing anguish deep in the pit of her stomach.

'You young girls are all the same,' he commented disparagingly. 'You're so naïve. You sleep with a man once and then think that gives you some special hold over him, some special privilege. But it doesn't. Particularly a man like Vann. I don't like to have to tell you this, sweetheart, and I'm sorry about your sister—we all are—but he was just trying to make you feel better. He probably didn't mean to hurt your feelings. But if you come here, making yourself available...' His extended hands said it all. From his expression she knew exactly what he thought of her.

'It wasn't like that,' Mel uttered, wounded by his cold cruelty, the way he was reducing the tenderness she had shared with Vann to little more than sleaze.

'What did you think it was? The real thing between you two?' he sneered, looking, with his close-cropped hair, like a club bouncer, used to dealing with unwanted customers. 'When you're older you'll realise not to take these things so seriously. It wasn't a wise thing coming here. Vann has his career. You could make things bad for him—and yourself—if this got out. Think how it would look. Here.' He was rummaging in a back pocket. 'The least we can do is pay for your petrol home.'

She shrank away from the notes he was suddenly thrusting in front of her. She felt like a prostitute being paid off, or some greedy opportunist being settled with for no further hassle.

Had Vann discussed her with his manager? She just couldn't believe that Vann would have told him anything about last night. But Bern Clayton had already told her that she was naïve.

Refusing to accept that Vann would have done such a thing, she said, 'If he did mean it, he won't know where to find me. If I write my telephone number down, would you give it to him?'

'If he wanted to find you, he'd find you all right. Numbers wouldn't be necessary.'

'Please,' she appealed, feeling a cold desolation washing over her.

He shook his head again, his expression suddenly one of pitying resignation.

'I'll give it to him,' he said. 'But that's all I can do. Leave it on the table before you go.'

So she had, enclosing not only her number but also a few brief lines, which, even now, nearly fourteen years on, made Mel cringe to remember. As did her foolish behaviour that night with Vann. It was something she didn't even want to think about, let alone admit to anyone else. She hadn't even told Karen everything when her friend had asked.

She had told her, of course, what had happened to her sister and about confronting Vann. She had even mentioned how she had collapsed from exhaustion, and had had to spend the night in his hotel. But it had been easy to withhold the full facts from her friend as Karen had been rendered speechless by the whole train of events. Because, of course, shortly after Kelly had died, unable to withstand the shock, Sharon Ratcliffe had succumbed to the same heart defect that had claimed her youngest daughter, leaving a stunned, bereft Mel to cope alone.

Six months later she read that the group had disbanded. She never heard from Vann Capella again.

CHAPTER FOUR

JONATHAN was chatting with several clients when Mel stepped out on to the terrace that evening. Because of her migraine she had skipped dinner, but now she had recovered enough to shower and dress for what was basically a welcome party for their guests.

'Mel. Glad you could make it.' Jonathan sought her out before she could join his group, his grey eyes wandering appreciatively over her.

Because lounge suits and cocktail wear were the order of the day, Mel had chosen a pale green crêpe de Chine strappy top with a low, curving neckline and sensuously fluid matching trousers that moved against her legs like a breath of air. Her hair she had left loose in a cascade of brilliant auburn, the overall impression, with her dark curling lashes, softly shadowed green eyes and burnished lips, one of unquestionable femininity.

'You look stupendous,' Jonathan breathed, impressed. 'You haven't got a drink. Let me rectify that.' He gestured to a passing waiter, deposited a cool glass of champagne into her hand.

'I need to talk to you—before anyone else does,' he said in a lowered voice, which explained his reason for singling her out, she realised, following his rather stealthy glance over her shoulder.

Her heart missed a beat when she saw Vann's dark figure dominating a small group of clients on the other side of the terrace. He had told Jonathan earlier that he couldn't make it for dinner, so she hadn't expected him to be here for the party. She could hear his companions laughing, see them hanging on his every word, totally absorbed in whatever it was he was saying, and Mel turned back to Jonathan, feeling as though someone had just sucked the air out of her lungs as she tried to make sense of whatever it was he was telling her.

'...overheard Vann telling Squire that he's testing the water with us as it were, obviously looking for reasons why he shouldn't stick with the agencies he's been used to.'

'It's his prerogative. He doesn't have to use us if he doesn't want to,' Mel responded, catching on. In fact, things would be far less complicated, for her at any rate, she thought, if he didn't. 'Only joking,' she assured Jonathan quickly nevertheless, seeing the dismayed look on the MD's face. Heywood was a huge national company, and he'd been worried about losing the account for weeks. 'We're the best, and all these people here—' she indicated the happily conversing élite of their clientele with a gesture of her glass '—know it.'

'And it's your job to make sure Vann does.'

A fine auburn eyebrow arched. 'Mine?' Beneath Mel's composed veneer a little twinge of pain made itself felt at the point where her head had throbbed earlier. 'Why mine? I would imagine *the* Mr Capella would be used to dealing only with top brass. You know, like yourself.' She was trying to sound casual, as though she didn't care one way or the other, when in fact the thought of having to involve herself with Vann any more than she had to was in danger of throwing her into a blind panic.

'Oh, come on, Mel,' Jonathan urged with a hint of impatience. 'Use your loaf. He might speak impeccable English, but he is half Italian with hot Latin blood in his veins. Therefore he's not averse to a pretty face. Besides...' he leaned towards her so as not to be overheard by anyone else, so close that anyone watching might have thought they were an item '...I think he fancies you.'

'Don't be ridiculous!' Mel returned hotly, disconcerted as well as outraged by what Jonathan was intimating.

'Be nice to him,' he warned.

Head cocked, Mel eyed her friend and colleague suspiciously. 'Nice to him?'

'You know what I mean.'

'I'm not sure I do,' she said.

'Oh, come on, Mel. Stop being deliberately obtuse. I don't mean sleep with the man. You don't really think I'm asking you to do that?'

She wasn't sure what he was asking, only realising that since meeting Vann here today she had been half-hoping she could use the shield of Jonathan's friendship to protect her from the man and from her own mixed feelings about him. But now it looked as though she wasn't even going to be able to do that.

'Just use that blazing charm of yours. You haven't exactly been in a rush to stick around and show him the sort of hospitality his reputation warrants and it's too important an account to louse up. Just don't do anything to ruffle his feathers,' he advised.

Taking a sip of champagne, hoping its effects would steady her nerves, Mel murmured, 'Are we dealing with a peacock?' Flippancy was the only tool she could employ to hide her agitation.

'No,' Jonathan reminded her grimly. 'More a sharp-witted, hard-taloned bird of prey.'

A shiver ran down Mel's spine as a cascade of silver notes sounded from the live band that had started to play under the awning that shaded the windows of the luxurious lounge bar. Jonathan's depiction of the man was over the top, but so was her response to it, she decided.

'I'll do my job,' she told him flatly, just before the tall, thin, quiet-voiced Jack Slater intruded apologetically, obviously wanting to speak to Jonathan, and gratefully Mel eased out of their orbit, welcoming a few moments alone.

Several couples were dancing to the slow instrumental melody filling the night air. Others were standing or sitting in small groups around the scattered tables, drinking champagne.

Mel knew the right thing to do was to approach the group nearest her, offer them refills, make them feel special, as important as they were to the agency. But after that unsettling exchange with Jonathan, and the knowledge that he was placing the responsibility of saving the Heywood account squarely on her shoulders, she needed breathing space to gather her wits.

Sure no one was watching her, she covered the few feet to the edge of the terrace and, with both hands cupping her glass, rested her arms on the cool, polished wood of the balustrade.

The warm breeze caressed her bare shoulders, fanning the loose fire of her hair. Lamps, strategically placed, lit the steeply-terraced gardens, beyond which the dark rocks plunged to the sea. In the night-shrouded bay strings of lights from several large yachts cast silver streaks across the water, but these were nothing compared with the thousands of twinkling lights from every house and hotel that made Positano glimmer with a breathtaking fairytale quality.

A stream of red tail-lights moving along the otherwise unlit coast road caught her attention and she followed its progress away from the town, beyond the ridge of dark land that formed the village of Praiano on the next headland, until it was lost from view.

'What lonely traveller needs the Madonna watching over him when he has you?'

Mel swung round, almost spilling her champagne.

From a distance, in an immaculate dark suit, Vann had looked devastating. Now, at close quarters, with that strong black hair worn loose, and contrasting starkly with the pristine white shirt, he turned her insides to jelly. Flouting convention, yet again he was tie-less, the open V of his shirt revealing the hard contrast of his skin, and the dark, corded strength of his throat.

Needing all her will to drag her gaze away from him, Mel glanced upwards to the sightseeing spot on the road above the hotel where the coach parties stopped to admire the view and take photographs and where, from her vantage point, the illuminated statue of the Madonna—like so many Mel had seen on the roadside since coming to Italy—gazed serenely down on the fairy-lit resort below them.

'I'm fallible,' Mel responded, meeting his eyes. 'She isn't.'

'And to put his trust in you, a man could lose his way?'

He was joking, but there was cynicism in his voice, too. Pointedly, Mel said, 'It depends on the man,' and took a swift draught of her champagne.

That dark head dipped in acknowledgement. 'Have you been along that road you seemed to be viewing so wistfully? Wishing what?' he asked. 'That you could be far away from here having fun, instead of having to pander to the likes of people like me?'

He was smiling, but Mel guessed there was a shrewd calculation going on inside that sharp brain.

'Contrary to how it looked, I do enjoy being with my clients.' She flashed him one of her most flattering smiles. 'It was unforgivable, I know, but I just couldn't help being enticed over by the view. I'm sure no one noticed.' This with a sideways glance that showed her clientele still laughing, chatting obliviously amongst themselves. No one except you, she thought with a little shudder. 'And no,' she said, answering his question. 'I haven't been any further south than Positano.'

Something like mockery touched the firm line of his

mouth. 'You should,' he recommended. 'Praiano's worth a visit—as are all the villages from here to Amalfi. You must let me show you. It's among the most—if not *the* most romantic drive in the world.'

It sounded glorious, but his startling offer, along with that disturbing adjective he had used in connection with it, gave rise to every instinct of self-preservation within Mel.

'That's very kind of you, but I'll be far too busy for much sightseeing,' she answered, trying to inject the right amount of regret into her voice, trying to ignore that crazy little part of herself that ached to accept.

'Too busy to keep the clients happy?' That mockery was still there, tinged with what? The slightest admonishment? 'I thought that was the whole purpose of your being here. In fact, I wouldn't mind betting that that was what that little pep-talk you seemed to be getting from your boss just now was all about.'

'Wouldn't you?' Mel hid her startled surprise behind a wary smile. Had he noticed Jonathan's covert glances in his direction? She turned her back on the magical view and, uncomfortably aware of Vann following her back into the hub of the party, tossed over her shoulder, 'You could lose your money—betting on a conversation you couldn't possibly have heard from the other side of the terrace.'

'I didn't realise you'd noticed,' he said silkily.

Blast him! Mel thought, trying to equate her memory of the worldly, yet vulnerable young man to whom she had once given herself so freely with this steel-hard, speculative sophisticate.

'Body language.'

'What?' Weaving her way through the throng, she spared a smile for the matronly but elegant Maureen Squire who was just joining her husband and another couple at one of the round tables.

'Body language,' that deep voice repeated. 'It can tell one far more than mere words ever could.'

Amidst the laughter and conversation, Mel turned round to face him. She felt safer now she wasn't so alone with him, wondering why that word should spring so readily to mind. 'And what did our body language tell you?' she prompted, green eyes meeting blue with something of a challenge.

'That you're more than professional colleagues.'

'That's not true,' Mel protested without thinking, glancing automatically towards the attractive blond man. One could hardly call a couple of platonic dinners a raging affair!

'In that case, dance with me.'

The soft command brought her gaze darting upwards to meet those crushingly familiar features, her every instinct screaming at her to refuse.

He doesn't know who you are! Nor did she want him to find out, she realised. Any more than she wanted to acknowledge that, after all these years, despite his lack of interest in her before, despite her hard lessons and her maturity, she was still hopelessly drawn to him. But to make an excuse would seem rude, she decided. After all, she had unwisely spurned his offer to take her sightseeing. Besides, Jonathan had told her to be nice to him for the account's sake. Out of the corner of her eye she was aware of the MD, ostensibly listening to Jack while sending odd glances her way. She didn't want any arguments with Jonathan on top of everything else.

Straightening her shoulders, steeling herself for the inevitable, she saw Vann's mouth quirk in response.

'Do I take that to be a ''yes''?' he asked, much too clever for comfort, totally aware of what was going on.

She met those steely eyes with a coolness she was far from feeling. 'You're very astute.' To her own ears it sounded more like an accusation than a compliment.

'I have to be.' He was relieving her of her glass, discarding it on an empty table they had to pass to reach the other dancers. 'I promise you this won't hurt,' he stated softly, taking her in his arms.

But it will! her brain screamed chaotically as she felt the warmth of his hand against the small of her back, pressing her close to him. *It will! More than you know!*

'Relax.' His voice, so familiar, was like the sensuous purr of a jungle cat. 'You're so tense.'

That's because I can't cope with this! Mel wanted to cry out, despairing that he should notice, and for a fleeting moment had to close her eyes against the devastating sensations running through her.

They had only shared one night. Yet with the first combined movement of their bodies, hers was awakening to the conscious knowledge of his, all her senses straining in recognition of the whole man—the lithe economy of his movements, his latent strength, that sweep of dark shadow around his jaw, the long-forgotten musk of his skin. He had taken her to Paradise and back again and she had paid for it over and over; through her guilt and shame that she could have succumbed so easily to the man who had robbed Kelly of her life; through the knowledge that he could as easily discard and forget her. Through…

The sudden flexing of that arm around her brought her eyes flying open to see him steering her out of the path of Jack and Hannah, who had just joined the dancers. Jack looked awkward, slightly uncomfortable on the dance floor, Mel thought, her gaze returning to Vann. There was an almost indiscernible furrow between his eyes.

'So what is Mel short for?' he enquired casually, although she had a feeling he had wanted to ask something else. 'Melissa?'

She nodded and he repeated it, and she was reminded

with a cruel jolt of the first time he had spoken her name, when it had lingered on his lips like a sacred prayer.

'It's a beautiful name.'

'Thank you.'

'Like the woman herself.' Before Mel could say anything, caught off guard by his remark, he went on, 'You said it was your friend who was taking your daughter to Rome.'

It was something he must have overheard her telling one of the others at lunchtime. Nevertheless, his abrupt change of subject surprised her.

'Yes.'

'Do I take it then that there isn't a Mr Sheraton?' And, when she hesitated, instinct warning her against having him cross the boundaries of her private life, 'You aren't wearing a wedding ring,' he stated. 'I couldn't help but come to the conclusion that there isn't. Well, is there?' he pressed relentlessly.

For a moment it would have been so easy to lie. To claim the safety of a husband as protection against her own reckless attraction to this man and this very disconcerting situation in which she was trapped. But he could find out the truth from Jonathan or any of the others if he chose to, so, treading carefully, she answered, 'Not any more.'

'Or any other serious relationship for that matter, despite what illusions your boss might have to the contrary.'

The highlights in her hair danced like fire as she inclined her head to ask pointedly, 'What makes you say that?'

The music was soft and dreamy and more couples were dancing now, but Mel noticed nothing but how the terrace lights made the clean thickness of his hair gleam like polished jet, and how the shadows, as he moved, made an enigma of the planes and angles of his face, strengthening its beautiful austerity.

'The way you were looking at me down there in that restaurant the other day.'

Mel's heart seemed to come up into her mouth. Why did he have to mention that?

'I thought you were someone I knew,' she said unthinkingly, and immediately could have kicked herself. That path was far too ill-advised to go down.

'Do you look at all the men you think you know like that?' he enquired, his tone softly censuring.

'Like what?' she queried, abashed. She knew only too well.

'I think we're both adults. I don't think I need to spell it out for you. But I will if you want me—'

'No!'

'So you do know what I'm talking about.'

His mouth was twitching in sensual amusement, those shrewd eyes watching the colour deepen in her cheeks, probably noticing the tension too that made her skin feel as though it were being stretched across her face as she struggled to find a way to excuse her uncharacteristic behaviour that day.

'Look, I'm sorry if I gave you the entirely wrong message,' she stressed, battling for composure, 'but I wasn't looking at you in any particular way. Now, can we drop the subject?'

A masculine eyebrow lifted in mocking scepticism, but all he said was, 'Certainly,' his compliance surprising her. She couldn't imagine him giving up on anything that easily.

'Let's talk about you,' she said. 'You didn't mention earlier that we were on trial.' The champagne was starting to take effect, but it was more from being in his arms and the unsettling turn the conversation had taken that was making her unduly careless, loosening her tongue.

'It's no secret,' he said. 'I'm quite satisfied with the companies I've been using. I've got a lot at stake. I need to know I'm getting the best. Heywood has been losing a lot of money.'

'May I ask what decided you on putting yours into it? Why you're so determined to pull it out of the mire?'

'Austin's an old friend of mine. Shares have hit rock bottom, as you'll be aware. Call it tossing a lifeline to a vessel in distress. But I'm not totally altruistic. Naturally, I do have my own interests at heart.'

'Naturally,' Mel repeated. The boy who had spent his childhood tossed around like a ship in a storm, and then been the victim of corrupt management, hadn't turned his fortunes around by letting sentiment dominate his hard-headed thinking. He had given her help when she had needed it. Solace, too, she thought, with a deep ache somewhere around her ribcage, but then he had moved on.

'And are you saying that perhaps we didn't do enough to prevent them sinking so low?'

'No. I think their problems were down more to bad management within the division, coupled with a downward trend in the market-place for the type of product on offer. If so, I shall be looking at upgrading. Developing a whole new product if possible.'

'Then you aren't just a silent partner.' As only this morning Jonathan had said he was. 'You're going to be actively involved in getting the company back on its feet?'

His eyes, shielded by those thick lashes, travelled lazily down over the serious oval of her face. For a moment they rested on the burnished amber of her mouth, before taking in the creamy slope of her shoulders, the gentle swell of her breasts revealed by the low neckline and softly he murmured, 'I am now.'

She wondered at the meaningful way in which he said that. Of course he couldn't have meant since coming here. Since meeting her. Nevertheless, an uneasy excitement stirred within her.

'I hear your company's among the best,' he commented. 'Not to mention your own record of success. Having seen your presentation this morning, familiarized myself with how you do things, I can see why. How long have you worked for Harvey's?'

Mel explained, skimming briefly over her five-year career with them, when she had joined as a sales executive, until taking a salaried directorship just over two years ago.

He was an attentive listener, his concentration solely on what she was telling him.

'And before that?' he enquired when she had finished. Clearly, he didn't believe in leaving any stone unturned.

'I had Zoë,' she said cagily, reluctant to revert to the subject of her personal life with him. 'I split my time between studying and working at home. Typing. Helping with promotional work. Generally keeping the wolf from the door. When she was old enough to go to school, I was able to devote more time to getting my career underway.'

'So...your husband's been off the scene for a long time.'

She hadn't intended to say anything to make him think she had done it all alone. Maybe it had been something in the tone of her voice, she thought. She hadn't set out to deliberately mislead him either, but she had, she realised, releasing the breath she wasn't aware she had been holding. She didn't know whether to feel grateful or ashamed. A bit of both, she decided when, taking her silence for affirmation, he went on, 'What happens to your daughter when you're working? Or are there other Karens in England waiting to whisk her off at a moment's notice?'

Something in his tone needled her, had her returning somewhat defensively, 'I spend as much time with her as I can. And I always make sure it's quality time. But I have to work to provide and Zoë knows that. I arrange my holidays around hers and, with the help of friends who also have children her age, we work something out. Besides, she's an independent child. She hates being tied to my apron strings.'

He laughed. 'Something I can't entirely envisage around that trim waist of yours.'

Mel felt her whole body tensing, suddenly conscious that the flimsy top, which only just reached the waistband of her trousers, had made it all too easy for his hand to slip beneath. She could feel that strong, warm hand against her lower back, feel it as erotically as when she had been naked with him…

Battling to bring her assailed senses under control, she said accusingly, 'You think I'm a hard-nosed career woman? With no time for a home and family?' Anger flared in her eyes, matching the burning highlights in her hair. 'Are you criticising me?' she enquired tetchily, unable to contain her pique because of the effect he was having on her.

Shadows chased across his face as they moved to the gentle music. 'I wouldn't dream of it,' he said. 'I admire what you do. What you've achieved under obviously very difficult circumstances. It's commendable. Shows courage and determination.'

'But?'

'Does there have to be a ''but''?' he enquired smoothly.

There did, although he wasn't admitting as much, pulling her closer to steer her out of the path of another dancing couple.

Her nostrils dilated, greedy for the masculine scent of him, her body responding to the delirious thrill of his nearness. Being of Italian descent, he carried the blood of a very family orientated culture, which alone could engender his disapproval of her way of life. But, recalling what she did know about his background, she knew that there were other reasons for the high moral stance he was refusing to voice. She could almost feel the censure in the compression of his mouth, in the taut, uncompromising line of his jaw.

'You think it isn't an ideal situation for a child?' she went on, still defensive. 'That I wouldn't have liked something better for mine? Any mother would,' she added emphatically. 'But sometimes it just doesn't work out that way.'

'I was only surmising that it must be tough—combining a job like yours with motherhood—single-handedly,' he said in more placating tones.

'It's had its moments.'

'I can imagine.'

Can you? she thought with bitter poignancy. Could he know what it was like nursing childhood illnesses? To scrape and save and eke out an existence as she had done during those early harrowing years? Working all hours of the day and night between poorly paid jobs, swotting for her degree?

'So how old is she?' he asked. 'No. Let me guess. Around twelve. Right?'

Lifting her chin, Mel hesitated with a blind stab of pain at her temples. But, considering the length of time until Zoë's birthday, she pulled a face and said, 'Only just.'

'Only just twelve?' His strong features were crossed by amused curiosity. 'Or only just right?'

Warning bells were clanging inside Mel's head. She didn't want to be talking to him like this. He hadn't recognised her, but the longer she was with him the greater the chance of his linking her to that distraught teenager who had behaved so badly with him. So, with a nervous little laugh, losing what confidence she had, she said, 'It amounts to the same thing, doesn't it?'

A line appeared momentarily between those dark brows. Could he tell how keyed up she was? she wondered. But then he nodded and, with a rather speculative look, said, 'I suppose it does,' and let it go.

The music had stopped. Around them people were applauding the three-piece band. Automatically, they both joined in.

'Well, I really should mingle,' Mel was pleased to be

saying as the applause died away. A quick glance towards Jonathan showed him watching them both. For all his advice about her being nice to Vann, he wasn't looking particularly happy. 'I'll look forward to discussing your ideas during the coming week, but if there's anything you need before then—any questions you want to ask—'

'Well, yes,' he said, cutting across her invitation to call her or any member of her team. 'There is one.'

'Oh?' She looked up at him with a forced smile, immensely relieved, now that he had released her, to be back on a more formal footing with him.

'Have we met before?'

The unexpectedness of his question hit her like a bombshell. Under his hard examination she felt her stomach muscles knotting, her throat clog with more than just the humiliation of being recognised. But, if he couldn't remember, then she wasn't going to tell him, was her cowardly thought, and on a tight little laugh she said, 'I think I would have remembered if we had.'

For a moment those steely eyes seemed to strip away the layers of her composure, exposing her as the sham she was beneath the fine gauze of her defences. But then, mercifully, John Squire came up and slapped a hand on Vann's shoulder, asking if he would join them, and Mel quickly excused herself. As she left them to it, she wondered how many more episodes like that her nerves could stand.

CHAPTER FIVE

JONATHAN was in a petulant mood the following morning as he found Mel finishing a light breakfast alone, beside one of the open windows in the long, sunny dining room.

'I know I recommended that you were nice to him,' he began without any preamble, occupying the chair immediately opposite hers. 'But don't you think you were carrying things a bit too far? You even had Maureen Squire commenting on what a perfect couple you made,' he complained, clearly jealous.

'I only danced with him,' Mel stressed, wanting to forget about Vann Capella, how it felt being in his arms, those mortifying few moments afterwards. She was glad he wasn't staying at the hotel. That his villa was just along the coast so that he wasn't always around like their other clients to unsettle her, perhaps press the point of the drive she had successfully managed to wriggle out of. 'All things considered, I couldn't very well refuse, could I?' She cast a sidelong glance out of the window. Way down, on one of the terraces, someone was setting out the sun beds around the deserted blue oblong of the pool.

'You weren't just dancing. You obliterated the rest of us. What were you talking about so intently anyway?'

Mel felt like telling him to mind his own business. She had enough troubles on her plate without this conflict of interests with Jonathan to contend with as well. But it was his business. Or partly, anyway, she reminded herself, and so she said, 'His new ad campaign. Oh, and Zoë. We talked about Zoë.' It struck her suddenly that Vann had shown comparatively more interest in her daughter during the space of a few minutes than Jonathan had in all the time she had known him. 'Anyway, he'd know if I were leading him on just to keep Heywood's custom. He isn't stupid. Don't underestimate him, Jonathan.'

'Don't you either,' he warned, helping himself to a carton of fruit yoghurt from a selection in the centre of the table. 'He'd swallow you for breakfast and then spit you out without turning a hair.'

Tell me about it, Mel thought, glad when Hannah, dressed similarly to herself in shorts and sun top, chose that moment to come and ask whether she fancied a stroll into Positano.

As it turned out, it was just what she needed, Mel decided later, because the endless steps leading down between the houses and linking the quiet lanes—a shortcut from the winding mountain road—demanded all their concentration to negotiate. But eventually the steep route brought them, with a momentum that had them laughing, down into the very heart of the bustling little resort.

'What was it like to dance with him?' Hannah shook her by suddenly asking when they were sitting sipping fruit punches outside one of the beach cafés.

'Who?' Mel parried, stirring the beverage needlessly with her straw.

Hannah laughed. 'You know very well.'

Glancing at a slow-moving queue of tourists on the quayside boarding the ferry for Sorrento, Mel shrugged, feigning nonchalance. 'I was merely doing my job.'

Fairer-skinned even than Mel, the younger girl's face showed signs of a little too much sun, Mel noted, as Hannah laughed and said, 'Give me a job like yours any day. I'd sacrifice a year's salary for it!'

'Would you?' A wan smile hid Mel's inner anguish. She couldn't tell Hannah that because of Vann she had sacrificed far, far more than that.

'You weren't doing too badly yourself with Jack,' Mel

reminded her, needing to change the subject. She knew Hannah liked the amiable young sales manager, evident from the way that ultra-pale skin reddened still more.

As they walked up through the vine-covered arbour of the town's pedestrian thoroughfare they saw local artists displaying their talents beneath bright blossoms of bougainvillaea. Here, numerous craft bazaars and endless boutiques provided a shopper's paradise all the way from the main street, down past the cathedral with its imposing majolica dome—visible from any point of the town—to the last steep steps leading to the harbour cafés and the sea.

Reaching the point just past the main square where the hotel courtesy car collected guests who didn't fancy the arduous walk back, they both turned as a horn beeped loudly behind them. It was a battered little red Fiat, driven, Mel realised, by one of the waiters she had seen eyeing Hannah at the party.

'He wants to know if we'd like a lift,' the blonde told Mel, having rushed forward as soon as the car pulled up. Already the young man was opening the front passenger door.

'You go on,' Mel said. She had noticed a skirt in one of the exclusive little boutiques on their descent into town earlier and had promised herself a closer look on her return. 'I want to do some more shopping. I can get the bus back later.' And, to the pleased-looking Italian, 'Thanks, anyway.'

'Well, he's no Vann Capella,' said Hannah, climbing in. 'But beggars can't be choosers.' Mel was still laughing as the little car screeched away.

Taking her time, she reached the shop and was deliberating over a gold and bronze gypsy-style skirt that was hanging with a number of other bright garments around the doorway, when a voice behind her said, 'It wouldn't suit you more if it had been made for you. And the same garment would cost you twice as much in New York or Rome.'

Mel pivoted to see Vann smiling down into her face, the sheer impact of his presence bringing dismay and excitement warring together inside her.

'You—you weren't at the hotel this morning,' she said, trying to ignore that aura of strength and vitality about him, but realising hopelessly that she sounded as though she had been thinking about him.

'I had some business in town.' His eyes ran unashamedly over the strappy cotton top that showed off the roundedness of her breasts, the lemon shorts that displayed too much smooth, golden leg. But fortunately the middle-aged shopkeeper was approaching them, offering her help in heavily accented English. Vann responded in fluent Italian.

'I've told her you'll buy it.'

Mel looked at him in amazement. 'Do you always make up other people's minds for them?'

His mouth compressed in amusement. 'It saves a lot of time. Apart from which, I never could mistake that longing in a woman's eyes.'

I'll bet you couldn't! Mel thought, guessing that he probably hadn't meant it in the way it had sounded. But his presence was far too disturbing, the memory of last night, of that other night of passion she had spent in his arms, causing such a kick of desire in her that she felt her breasts tighten in undeniable arousal against her skimpy top, recognised the throb of need deep in her loins.

She couldn't look at him as she went up to the counter to pay for her purchase.

'*Signore*…' The woman was speaking so quickly that, with her limited knowledge of the language, Mel couldn't possibly understand. She looked questioningly at Vann.

'She wants to know if I'd like to purchase a complementing piece of jewellery for the love of my life,' he translated, still looking amused. Smiling, the shopkeeper was holding up a delicately crafted gold chain.

'I trust you put her straight. That we're not an item,' Mel retorted, too unsettled by the whole situation to share his amusement.

'Who said she was talking about you and me?'

Two bright spots of colour invaded Mel's cheeks. Of course, she thought, brought firmly down to size.

A dispiriting unease crept through her, which was ludicrous, she told herself firmly. After all, until the other day he had been safely buried in the past.

'Why do I get the impression you like wrong-footing people?' she tossed up at him as they were leaving the shop, the brightly coloured bag dangling from her fingers.

'I don't. Only when the music's playing a waltz and they try to tango with me.'

Mel's pulse quickened. 'Oh?' she queried cagily as they stepped into the sun-baked street. It was surging with people. 'I thought we were pretty much in step last night. Did I bruise your toes or something?'

'Forget it,' he drawled. 'Are you going back to the hotel?' And, without waiting for an answer, 'Come on. I'll give you a lift.'

His car was the black Aston Martin she had seen from the conference room window the previous day, parked in the small multi-storey car park across the street. The smell of its pale leather upholstery impinged on her nostrils as she sank into her seat, but her mind was screaming for a way out as the car growled out of the car park, climbing the hill out of town.

He was no fool, she thought. He knew she was hiding something from him, even if he didn't know what it was.

All you have to do is tell him! she urged herself. But she couldn't. She'd feel humiliated. An utter fool!

Common sense, however, warned her that he had known

deceit once before, and that he probably wouldn't take too kindly to finding himself a victim of it a second time.

I can't do this! she thought, panicking, wondering what Jonathan would say if he realised that putting responsibility for the Heywood account on her shoulders was like throwing a match into a powder keg. But the only alternative was to back out of the conference and the only way she could do that was to tell Jonathan the truth.

But that was out of the question, she decided, and, even if it weren't, she couldn't let this situation affect her professionalism. She valued her job and her clients, and she had no intention of letting one long-forgotten night—at least where Vann Capella was concerned—ruin all that she had worked for.

She was glad when they had climbed the hill and the car was swinging on to the hotel's sloping drive. The statue of the Madonna stood white and serene on her pedestal as they passed it, looking seaward over the vista, hazy from the midday heat.

'Apart from a brief talk this afternoon which, I'm afraid, I can't attend,' Vann said, applying the handbrake, 'I see from your agenda that there are no more talks or presentations taking place this week.'

Mel breathed an inward sigh. Was he saying he wouldn't have been able to attend those either? Did that mean she could unwind at last?

'That's right. You can all take time off for good behaviour.' Relief made it easy to laugh.

'In that case, as you aren't tied up, you won't mind if I monopolise your time tomorrow to toy around with a few ideas I have in mind for Heywood. You can give me the benefit of your expert advice and we can take in the coast at the same time. I'll pick you up at nine,' he stated, and that was it. Settled.

Mel felt as if she had been bulldozed as he drove away.

* * *

'You're kidding!' Karen exhaled when Mel rang to check up on Zoë the following morning, then went on to tell her friend about the bizarre coincidence in meeting Vann, that she was going to be out with him for most of the day.

'Wow!' Karen continued to exclaim, unaware of her friend's raging apprehensions. 'And I thought you were ringing to tell me Jonathan had asked you to move in with him and that you'd accepted.'

'Hardly,' Mel answered with a grimace.

'Still, he can't be very pleased,' her friend commented.

He hadn't been when Mel had told him, questioning her rather huffily as to why Vann couldn't discuss his affairs there at the hotel like everyone else. Mel had wanted to point out that he had virtually thrown her into Vann's arms in the first place, but decided to bite her tongue. Now all she simply said was, 'It's business, Karen.'

'Yeah?'

'Yes,' Mel stressed, but her friend wasn't listening.

'Wait until I tell Simon,' she enthused excitedly. 'Not to mention your daughter. She scarcely talked about anything else on the journey back. Do you want a word? She's sitting here on the floor watching— Oh no, she isn't. She—'

From Karen's abrupt silence it was clear Zoë hadn't waited before grabbing the phone. Now a rush of envy and disbelief met Mel's ears.

'You're never going out with him! Why couldn't *I* have stayed in Positano? You always get all the fun,' Zoë wailed. 'It's not fair!'

Quietly Mel reminded her daughter that she had expressly requested a week shopping with Karen in Rome, and that they would have seven fun days together when Mel came to collect her at the weekend, hiring a car and showing her more unexplored parts of Italy.

She came off the phone, however, feeling as though she

had compromised in one battle only to have to face another. This time with herself.

Still in her silk negligée, the cool femininity of her new skirt beckoned from the wardrobe, but after what Vann had said about it yesterday she had no intention of wearing anything that would give him the wrong message. Besides, she was going along with too much of what he wanted already, she thought hopelessly, donning a simple cotton wraparound skirt in a navy and turquoise print with a matching sleeveless shirt which she left open over a turquoise camisole.

Nevertheless, she couldn't contain the violent leap of her pulse when, waiting downstairs among the soft sofas and lush green plants around the reception area, she saw Vann's car pull up outside.

She reached the door just as he was pushing it open.

'*Buon giorno*,' he greeted her, turning her bones to jelly, unaware of how his softly-spoken Italian affected her. Or maybe he was, she thought, feeling that lethal blend of charisma and virility drawing her to him like a potent lure.

The pale grey T-shirt he wore with loose-fitting light trousers hugged his broad shoulders, accentuating the hard muscles of his chest. His hair gleamed black above that intellectual brow, accentuating the strong nose, the prominent bones of his cheeks and jaw.

'*Buon giorno*,' she returned, smiling, aware of his eyes wandering lazily over her, feeling the breeze fan her face, stirring the bright tendrils she had failed to capture in her loosely swept-up hair as she stepped out into the equally bright morning.

'You're probably the very first woman who's never kept me waiting,' he congratulated her, opening the passenger door.

'Did you think I would?' She watched him move around the bonnet, as lithe and supple as a great hunting animal. 'I'm a businesswoman, Vann. I learnt a long time ago that time is of the essence, and that to keep someone waiting is costly as well as rude.'

'Do you measure everything in terms of time and money?' he asked across the car's gleaming bodywork. It looked dark and sleek and powerful, just as he did.

'When I'm working, certainly. I would have thought a man in your position would know the importance of that.'

'Oh, indeed.' But he appeared to be mocking her as he joined her in the car. 'Let go, Mel.' His voice was suddenly soft, his features serious. 'Relax for a few hours.' Under his skilled direction the Aston Martin purred into life. 'That's the secret of succeeding. Work to the limit if necessary. But play as hard as you work.'

Feeling oddly chastened, Mel settled back against the pale leather, trying to do as he suggested while the car bore them down the winding mountain road and into the town once again.

The woman in the boutique where Mel had purchased her skirt the previous day was standing in her doorway. She waved to them as they passed. They both waved back.

'She recognised us. Or you,' Mel amended, thinking the latter more likely.

'She should. Her husband and I go back a long way,' Vann told her.

So they were probably used to seeing him with no end of different women, Mel thought, remembering their conversation in the shop the day before. Refusing to think about that, or anything concerning his private life, she absorbed herself instead in the sights and sounds of the popular little resort.

There was only one narrow road through and, just like yesterday, holidaymakers, ambled along it, walking in the road, browsing in shop windows, cameras hanging from shoulders. Several turned now and then to admire the sleek lines of the car. Someone laughed, shouting something in

Italian to someone else across the street. Car horns sounded, bringing Mel's attention suddenly to what was going on ahead.

They had met a little bubble of congested traffic, through which one of the town's single-decker blue buses was trying to manoeuvre. A small dog, standing on the footwell of the stationary motor scooter immediately in front of them suddenly hopped off, stretched its little legs with an interested sniff around the surrounding area and, as the traffic ahead started to move again, hopped back on with such precision timing it had both Mel and Vann laughing aloud.

'That would never be allowed in England!' she breathed, amazed.

'I'm not sure it's entirely legal here.' He grinned, amusement lessening the severity of those brooding features. He looked younger, more approachable somehow.

He turned suddenly and caught her smile, his blue eyes searching and intense. 'That's better,' he remarked, echoing her own thoughts about him, before giving his concentration to the road again.

Within minutes they had left the town behind them, travelling along a highway gouged out of the rocky cliffs. On their side of the road, unprotected by any railings, the cliff edge dropped away, plunging dramatically to the sea-washed boulders hundreds of feet below.

'What do they call that island?' Mel asked, glancing back towards Positano and the dark mound of land jutting out of the aquamarine water. A rich man's heaven. 'Does it have a name?' Someone at the hotel had told her that it had once belonged to the famous Russian ballet dancer, Rudolf Nureyev.

'It's one of several and they're called "the Sirenuse", or "Galli isles".' He spread tanned fingers contemplatively on the steering wheel before saying, translating for her, 'The Cocks. Roosters. So named because a sorcerer who was rather partial to fowl once agreed to build a castle for the local king in exchange for all the roosters in Positano. The king saw to it that they were all slaughtered and sent to the sorcerer, but one young girl didn't want to give up her rooster and so she hid it under her bed. Of course, when it crowed the next morning, the sorcerer, thinking the king had betrayed him, abandoned the project, which is why Positano has no castle.'

'Somehow,' she breathed huskily, with an unintentionally provocative glance at him from beneath her dark lashes, 'I think you're having me on.'

His eyes met hers for just a fraction of a second, but long enough to ignite a spark of something exciting and dangerous in Mel. 'Now why would I do that?' His mouth was twitching as he turned his attention to the road again. 'These old wives' tales often contain an element of truth.'

'OK, so it's true!' Mel laughed. She hadn't felt this lightheaded in a long time. It was so good to be with him; it seemed so right, joking like this. Not at any time, since the day she had forced herself to accept that she'd never hear from him again, had she ever thought it possible. Despite her better judgement, she wanted to make the most of it. 'So what happened to the young girl?'

'The girl?' One of those broad shoulders lifted. 'Who knows? She wasn't important to the story.'

It was a flippant exchange—about a legend—but those dismissive words touched a raw nerve in Mel.

'I would have thought she was of paramount importance,' she strove to continue in the same light-hearted vein, but a sudden chill had settled around her heart.

Don't get on a too familiar footing with him, she warned herself. You aren't here to enjoy yourself with him. The fact that she had an overwhelming desire to do so didn't come into the equation. She hadn't been important enough for him to want to see her again all those years ago, understandably perhaps. She had meant nothing to him, after all. But even telling herself that at the time hadn't prevented the knowledge hurting beyond belief as, surprisingly, it still chafed now. And, if he did guess who she was, then she would have to face the double humiliation of his not only remembering what had happened between them, but realising she had misled him solely to cover up the shame she was still suffering because of it, and what could be more humiliating than that?

She'd be a fool to let him get under her skin a second time, she berated herself. Especially when she was in such control of her own life now—her own destiny. Her mother's life had been complicated in the extreme, and Mel was determined not to allow herself to be let down by men in the same way. She and Zoë were doing fine on their own, and that was how things were going to stay.

'You're looking very fierce.'

Vann's quiet observation shook her out of her disturbing reverie.

'Am I?' she responded, tension knotting her usually genial features. 'It's just all this…' A sweep of her arm indicated the breathtaking beauty of their surroundings. 'I've got a job taking it all in.' That part at least was true.

She couldn't remember having been on such a thrilling drive before and could understand now why he had referred to it as the most romantic in the world. The winding road, little more than two cars' widths in places, passed through white villages splashed with the reds and pinks of geranium, oleander and bougainvillaea. On their left hand side the mountains peered down like awesome giants, dominating everything over which they loomed. The lane in which they were travelling still hugged the cliff edge, where vineyards and citrus orchards and slumbering luxury villas with their clear blue pools, ornate balconies and bright shutters clung to the rocky coast. Here and there a sandy cove harbouring small boats could be reached by countless narrow steps leading between the houses, down through verdant gardens and olive groves to the very edge of the sparkling sea.

'I've never seen anything so beautiful,' she said.

'No,' he agreed rather heavily. And, when she darted a questioning glance in his direction, she realised from the mere meeting of their eyes that he wasn't talking about the scenery at all.

She looked quickly away, an insidious heat stealing through her. Careful, she warned herself again. Then let out a nervous little scream as a coach, coming straight at them over the white line of the northbound lane, forced Vann to steer sharply, bringing them precariously close to the cliff edge.

'Relax,' he advised, amused by her flushed cheeks and her tremulous little laugh. 'You're perfectly safe.' But she knew that already.

The Aston Martin's tyres seemed to suck the road and Vann's driving was impeccable—unlike the reckless, far too-talkative taxi driver who had terrified both Zoë and herself on the journey down from Naples. Mel trusted his judgement implicitly and those strong, capable hands turning the wheel. Those long, beautifully tapered hands that had once stroked and caressed her body, stamping their mark on her to such a degree that the experience had spoilt her for any other man, because no other man had ever quite been able to measure up...

The memory of that night rose, unbidden and unashamedly, assailing her mind and body with an acute hunger she didn't want to feel. But, against her prior warnings, she knew an immense joy at having shared this brief time with him, dizzy now, but from a surfeit of excited emotion rather than from the height at which they were travelling.

He started talking then about his ideas to salvage the company he was funding; ways to improve its image beside its competitors. He spoke with a knowledge of marketing and consumer psychology that left no doubt as to his expertise and the foresight that had earned him the hard-won success to which he had referred earlier.

In turn, he listened to her ideas, evaluating them against his own, applauding her suggestions in a way that filled her with an absurd pleasure, and, from the way he invited her to enlarge upon most of the concepts she was putting forward, she knew he was impressed.

They stopped for coffee in Amalfi. Set at the mouth of a deep gorge, it was the principal town along the coast, with an impressive cathedral presiding over red-roofed white houses and a trio of jetties reaching out into the glittering bay.

Tucking into deep wedges of lemon cake, they were still talking business when the waiter brought them their second cappuccino under the flapping canopy of the crowded beachside café.

'We make a good team,' Vann remarked, with a satisfied firming of his mouth. 'Perhaps I should engage you myself.'

He was only joking. Even so, as she savoured the tangy lemon icing, Mel's heart skipped a beat.

'You're just one of a number of clients with whom I'm happy to share my expertise,' she uttered amiably, trying to sound businesslike, trying not to appear so ridiculously affected by the thought of sharing anything with him, because she was. 'I love my job. You'd have to pay me a pretty hefty wage,' she went on to assure him dryly, 'to seduce me away.'

He looked at her over the steam of his cappuccino, those long fingers absently toying with a spoon in the delicious white froth.

'Who said anything about a seduction?' he drawled, and there was nothing vague about the way those penetrating eyes captured and held hers.

'I was speaking figuratively,' Mel stressed, disconcerted by the more intimate turn the conversation had taken. From the way his mouth quirked, he noted the tremor in her voice, the flush beneath the translucent freshness of her skin.

'How old are you, Mel?'

The simple question threw her. 'Thirty-one.' There was implied amazement in the arching of a thick eyebrow. 'How old did you imagine?' She had already worked out that he would be thirty-six.

'I guessed you had to be,' he said, 'to have a twelve-year-old daughter. Even if you do look less than twenty-five.'

Mel pulled a wry face, her senses unconsciously absorbing the sounds of conversation around them, the hiss of steam from the espresso machine at the far end of the café. 'Everyone says the same thing. I keep a portrait in the attic.'

Laughter creased the corners of his eyes. 'So the effects of all your sins are absorbed by the painting while you remain young and pure?'

'You like Oscar Wilde?'

'I admire his wit.'

'Oh, for a fraction of it!' Mel found she was agreeing, hugging a secret pleasure in the knowledge that they shared a literary interest. 'Anyway, who says I'm so young and pure?'

'Aren't you?' He smiled meaningfully. 'So I was wrong comparing you with the Madonna.'

'Very misguided,' she murmured, smiling back with unmindful provocation as she picked up her cup. The froth was soft and cool compared with the surprisingly hot coffee underneath.

'Careful,' Vann warned swiftly, but she had already burnt her tongue.

How could she keep her mind on anything? she despaired, her mouth smarting. With him sitting opposite her looking like the treacherous seducer in some Italian movie? Or some sculpted god of strength and virility with that aura of power he exuded and that disciplined fitness that had made every female head turn when they had walked to this table earlier?

She was no less immune, Mel thought, trying, as laughter from another table drew his attention for a moment, to drag her gaze away from his arresting profile.

Too late, though; he turned back and caught her hopeless fascination for him. His mouth tugged in the subtlest of acknowledgements.

'What happened with you and Zoë's father?'

'What?' Agitatedly she looked down at her own cappuccino, spooning the froth as he had done. 'Oh...' Still not looking at him, she shrugged. 'It didn't work out.'

'How long were you together?'

Mel placed her spoon back into her saucer, her movements slow and measured. She didn't want to talk about past relationships. 'No time at all,' she admitted at length. 'He left before Zoë was even born.'

Surprise etched the strong masculine features. 'So he didn't know her?' And when Mel shook her head, 'That's tough,' he said with genuine understanding.

'It was my own fault. I was young and impetuous,' she said, wanting to drop the subject.

'Too young for commitment, that's for sure.' The deep tones were censuring. 'And you've never been tempted to settle down with anyone else?'

He was taking a lot for granted, but Mel decided it was best left that way. At the end of the week she would be back home. Back to her comfortable, suburban flat and her safe, practical, uncomplicated existence. Somehow, it didn't seem very thrilling.

'Why should I?' she quizzed. 'I've got a nice home. A great job. Zoë.'

Those blue eyes were coolly speculative. 'Is it enough?'

Was it? He was holding a mirror to her life, she realised, and she didn't like it.

'Yes,' she answered, rather too determinedly. 'Contrary to what society still might expect, not every woman's ultimate goal in life is to finish up with a husband. Mine certainly isn't.'

From the way his eyebrow cocked, her less than complimentary view of the matrimonial state had made its mark. Lifting his cup, however, all he said was, 'Not even for your child's sake?'

'I couldn't do it solely for that reason. I have to think what's right for me, too.'

'Over and above your child's security?' She wasn't sure whether that hard glitter in his eyes was disapproval or not.

'No,' she argued defensively, colour creeping up her throat. 'And she is secure.'

Suddenly the magic of the morning had gone, swept away by his uncomfortably probing questions, her annoyed response to them and by a little wave of guilt, too. Guilt which, in spite of all her declarations to the contrary, made her question, and not for the first time, whether she was in fact acting fairly in depriving Zoë of a surrogate father. Whether by her staying single her daughter had missed out on a great deal. She remembered the phone call that morning, how disappointed Zoë had sounded not to be here, her protestations of life being unfair, that her mother had all the fun, only compounding the guilt Mel felt, then and now.

It was that emotion, more than anything else, that had her throwing back at Vann, 'You really don't approve of my lifestyle, do you?'

'I don't know enough about it to approve or disapprove,' he said in more placatory tones. 'I've learnt enough, though, to realise that if anyone asks about it you come over all defensive.'

'I do not!' She knew that with that heated retort she was

only cementing his opinion, but her feelings about him—
about Zoë—were in too much danger of being laid bare to
respond in any other way.

'Blame my Italian side for making me believe that a child
is better off with two parents. It's my personal opinion that
he or she gets a more balanced view of life. But it is only
my opinion.'

'Well, you would think that, wouldn't you? Having—'

She broke off abruptly, realising her anger was making
her careless, wishing she had bitten off her sore tongue
when she saw him frown.

'Having…what?' he queried softly, sitting back, his cappuccino finished. As if he had a cast-iron stomach, Mel
thought distractedly.

Unnerved by the intensity of his regard, she lifted her cup
and gingerly took a sip of her coffee. It had cooled just a
little. Unlike me, she thought, feeling hot and sticky beneath
her brightly printed top and skirt.

'I'm not sure what I was going to say,' she bluffed. God!
How could she have been so stupid?

With an elbow resting on the back of his chair, Vann's
eyes had narrowed into slits, the stretched fabric of his T-
shirt emphasising his muscular chest, the broad shoulders
and strong upper arms.

'Where was it, Mel?'

Fazed by his question, she put down her cup, knocking
the little silver spoon out of her saucer. Quickly she retrieved it. It left a small brown stain on the creamy cloth.

'Where was what?' she asked cagily.

'Where was it we met before?'

CHAPTER SIX

THOSE shrewd eyes were so intent that she couldn't meet them.

Studying the small vase of yellow flowers in the centre of the table, she said with an affected little laugh, 'Have you known so many women that you can't remember the ones you've met from the ones you haven't?'

'Answer me,' he commanded quietly, dismissing her question with almost contemptuous scorn.

'Well, if we had known each other before…' eyes guarded, stalling for time, she lifted her small chin, censure masking the pain behind every fine feature as somehow she found the courage to say '…it wouldn't be doing a lot for my ego to think I could be so easily forgotten.'

'I wouldn't be human if I'd forgotten *you*,' he breathed.

Oh, but you have! cried an injured little voice inside her. OK, she might have been just a one-night affair. And he must have had scores of women since. But all that didn't make it any easier to bear!

'I'll bet you use that line on every woman,' she accused lightly in an attempt to keep a tight rein on her emotions, and gasped from the sudden grip of iron around her wrist.

She hadn't even seen him move. Such was the speed of his reactions. But his mouth was grim and fiery anger leapt in his eyes.

'I don't go in for useless flattery,' he argued. 'I only know that something flared between us down there in that restaurant the other day—that you felt it as strongly as I did—until I spoke to you—or until you realised who I was—and then you closed up like a limpet on a rock. Why?'

'I told you,' Mel uttered, feeling hopelessly out of her depth. 'You got the wrong impression…'

'Is that why your pulse is racing crazily beneath my fingers? Or are you going to tell me I've got the wrong impression about that, too?'

Her gaze dropped to the dark thumb sensuously massaging her comparatively pale flesh, beneath which a thin blue vein beat its merciless betrayal.

What could she say? she thought despairingly. Her responses to him were as reckless as they had been nearly fourteen years ago and, being an experienced, red-blooded male, he had recognised that fact, even if he hadn't recognised *her*.

'It's just chemistry,' she murmured on a derogatory little note.

'And you're determined to resist it to the bitter end.'

It wasn't a question, because he already knew the answer.

'I don't want any complications,' she admitted truthfully.

Those dark-fringed eyes seemed to dissect her before his thumb stilled on the frantic little pulse, his hand fell away and she was free.

'I'll get this,' he asserted harshly, seeing her intention to pay the bill the waiter had unobtrusively left while they had been talking, plucking it out of her reach.

'You're my client,' Mel protested, taking out her credit card.

'And therefore a tax deductible expense?'

His tone implied that he didn't like being regarded as such. But, still trembling from the shock of his touch and determined to keep things formal between them, she said nevertheless shakily, 'Something like that.'

'Put your purse away,' he ordered, and so incisively that she decided it best to obey. Her confusion made her clumsy, however, and as she was replacing the little piece of plastic some of the contents in the wallet section of her purse slid out—her driving licence, the business card supplied by the taxi driver who had brought her from Naples, a little gold booklet of English stamps.

She caught them all before they could get away from her. Vann, though, was picking up something from the floor.

'May I?' Without waiting for a reply, he turned the little photograph over. It was one of Zoë and herself, taken the previous summer during a weekend trip to Weymouth. It showed Mel in a green bikini. Zoë was in shorts and a crop-top, with a baseball cap turned round the wrong way hiding her sleek, dark auburn hair. Arms around each other, they were both grinning broadly at the camera.

'Someone offered to snap the two of us while I was trying to take a picture of Zoë,' Mel explained, suddenly deciding the bikini was far too revealing now beneath such intense male scrutiny. He seemed almost transfixed by it, those thick lashes lowered, his mouth and jaw chiselled with an emotion that seemed to hold him in thrall.

Quickly Mel grabbed the photo, stuffing it with the rest of her errant belongings back into her purse.

'Ready?' Vann asked tersely, getting up.

She wasn't. She was still putting her purse away and she hadn't finished her cappuccino but she nodded.

'Then let's go,' he said, tossing a couple of notes unceremoniously on to the plate containing the bill.

Scrambling to her feet, Mel caught a glimpse of his face as he ushered her out of the café. She thought he looked pale, tight-lipped, angry, and she wasn't sure why. She only knew that his mood had changed and simply put it down to his male ego being deflated.

Well, that isn't my problem, she thought, following him back to the car, and heard the echo of those words printed in that national newspaper she couldn't count how many lifetimes ago. *It wasn't his problem.* Words that had lured her to him. Words he had denied and which denial she had been so ready to believe. Which, in spite of everything, she still believed, she realised, with a little shiver of desolation that had everything to do with the past, she assured herself, not with the present. But her conviction fell into a chasm of such emptiness she knew it was a lie.

They walked in silence to the car park, a piazza between the outstretched arms of two jetties, reaching out into the sapphire sea.

Now, as they climbed into the blistering heat of the car, Vann started the engine and threw on the air-conditioning switch, the blast of its fans obviating the need for conversation.

He still looked grim, she thought, grappling with her seat-belt as he turned and flung an arm across the back of her seat.

To reverse out, she thought, then realised that was the last thing on his mind as that arm and one jerk of his knee brought her down across his lap, those hard hands turning her to lie face upwards to take the harsh invasion of his mouth.

She murmured a strangled protest, her hands against the unyielding wall of his body, trying in vain to push him away. But his mouth was insistent and unrelenting, forcing hers to open with a determination she was equally determined to fight.

Yet that musky male scent and the hard warmth of his body were aphrodisiacs in themselves, even without the punishing pressure of his mouth, and all at once her resistance snapped.

With a small moan of defeat, her arms slid up around him, drawing him down to her, inviting his kiss to deepen, to quell this need that she knew now had only been slumbering, this wanting that could only be assuaged by the driving energies of this one man.

Suddenly though he was releasing her, setting her back

upright again on her own side of the car. The fans were still blasting away and the air felt icy. With one swift, economical movement, Vann turned them off. The silence was almost deafening.

'So now we know, don't we?' he said, his voice as chilly as the air and, without waiting for an answer, reversed out of the space with an aggression that reflected his mood, leaving Mel shamed and stunned by the depths of her response.

Jonathan was leaning on the terrace railing, talking to Hannah and another member of his team. They were all wearing shorts and T-shirts, admiring the view. There had been a shower during the night and the air was sweet with the scent of jasmine and oleander as Mel walked over to join them.

'Have a nice time yesterday?' Jonathan asked when he saw her. His smile was cool, and Mel wondered if the other two detected that underlying edge to his voice because after their chorused, 'Good morning!' to her, they slipped unobtrusively away.

'Very constructive,' she responded, keeping her reply businesslike. He had been out when she had returned late the previous afternoon and at dinner they had been tied up with clients, after which Mel had made a hasty retreat to her room. 'In fact, he's bringing all the plans and sketches he's made of his own ideas for the new campaign today, so you'll be able to look at them if you want to. Don't worry, Jonathan.' She flashed him a brilliant, reassuring smile, honed from years of practice on anxious clients. 'He's still on the hook.'

He must have picked up on her unease because, with his eyes tugging suspiciously over the wild fire of her loose hair and her simple green cotton sun dress, he said, 'It isn't him I'm worried about. I just wonder who's trying to catch who.'

'What's that supposed to mean?' Mel asked with an oblique glance at him, wondering if he could detect something of her inner conflict.

'You spent rather a long time with him yesterday. I didn't imagine you'd be gone all day. I was hoping that perhaps we could have spent some time together. A few hours at least.' Those grey eyes continued to regard her. 'You look a bit peaky under that tan,' he remarked and, more caustically, 'Working you to the bone, is he? Getting his money's worth out of us?'

You could say that, she thought with a mental grimace. But not in the way you think. Just through the strain under which her unintentional deception had put her, even without her raging awareness of him as a man. He knew she was attracted to him, and she guessed that the sole reason for that kiss in his car yesterday had been to determine just how strongly. Which served her right, she thought, for that pompous little speech in the café about complications! And yet, after that, he hadn't referred to it or even tried to touch her again.

After leaving Amalfi, he had brought her back to Positano for a late lunch when further business was discussed and where, she discovered, he shared her own interest in good wine.

Yet as the meal had progressed he had brought the conversation round to a more personal level and she had found it increasingly difficult to evade his pointed questions. Questions about herself, her past, her family, which, coming from anyone else, would have been simply natural curiosity, but which, from him had seemed like an experiment to test her nerves! Also, behind his casual questions she had sensed a subtle yet very tangible cynicism towards her that she hadn't been aware of on the drive down, and she wondered if it all stemmed from that moment in the café in Amalfi when she had not only denied any prior knowledge of him, but had made it quite clear that she had no intention of getting involved with him. Which was probably why he had been so determined to show her she wasn't immune!

A typical male, she thought, but with a little shudder, too, because Vann Capella was far from typical. As she had warned Jonathan, the man wasn't stupid. He knew he had met her somewhere before, and all she could do was pray that she could get this week over with before he had worked out where. She was only glad she was going to be at the hotel today, and therefore would not have to be so alone with him. She didn't think her nerves or her emotions could have stood anything else.

'You are coping, are you?' She came back to the present to see Jonathan still studying her, his arms folded.

'Of course.' It took an effort but she summoned another bright smile. 'Have you ever known me not to?' And, to lead him off the track of her very personal anxieties, 'And you're right. Some time together would be nice.'

'Then I'm sorry I shall be taking her away. But you can have her back the moment I've finished with her, I promise.'

Mel's heart sank then doubled its rhythm as she swung round and met the impact of Vann's dark, brooding presence. In a white shirt and pale chinos, his hair tied in the usual way, he appeared totally in command beside the shorter, surprisingly flustered-looking MD.

'Oh, Vann. Good morning. No, that's fine,' he was saying in response to what Mel felt had been a purely superficial apology from Vann. 'Take all the time you want with her. Mel will be more than happy to accommodate you.' Jonathan's deference to their agency's top client made her skin prickle. There were times, she thought bitingly, when principles had to come before profit.

'I'll make sure I make full use of her,' Vann expressed, his lips faintly mocking in response to the look she sliced him. And, with a more than casual glance over her creamy gold shoulders, he said silkily, 'Are you ready, Mel?'

She heard the jangle of his car keys and only then realised that he was otherwise empty-handed. If he thought he was taking her off somewhere again…

In silently screaming protest she looked to Jonathan for help, and saw only pure accusation in his face.

He thinks I'm responsible for this, she realised, trying to match Vann's stride across the terrace. With her eyes boring into his broad back, she demanded, 'Where are we going?'

'I thought we'd look at the various papers back at the villa.' And when Mel, drawing level with him, shot him a glance that was purely contentious he went on, 'Don't worry. If you're concerned about your virtue I promise Quintina will protect you.' His housekeeper, she remembered from a conversation the day before.

'You're making a lot of promises this morning,' she reminded him as they walked through Reception together. The desk clerk nodded, acknowledging them. 'Do they include signing a contract with us if we satisfy all your requirements?'

'That depends.'

'On what?' she enquired, aware of the envying glances from two young women who had just stepped out of the lift, coveting the dynamic-looking man at her side.

He pulled open the swing door for her to step through, so close she could smell his cologne mingling with his more primeval masculine scent.

'I'm not easily satisfied,' he said.

His villa was a rambling, luxury residence only a short drive from Positano, with spectacular views over the sea.

Her first glimpse was of pristine white walls and meandering balconies, draped by the stark purple blooms of bougainvillaea. The grounds were steeply terraced, like most along the coast, where kitchen gardens gave on to a network of pathways and splashes of colour, through which sprawling shrubbery led on to citrus groves, and where, here and there, a classical stone statue basked in the fierce Mediterranean sun.

After the car's air-conditioning, the heat hit Mel like a furnace as Vann guided her up the wide, marble steps to the villa. It was pleasingly cool and airy inside.

Zoë would just love this, she thought, the youngster's complaints that her mother had all the fun still pricking at Mel with a little needle of self-reproach, as her eyes took in the features of the house. The beautifully carved staircase. The tasteful antiques and richly woven rugs and tapestries she could see through an archway leading to a sitting room. The flower arrangements that spilled out of baskets and jugs, which brought the freshness of the garden into the house, redeeming it from the starkly formal with their rustic simplicity.

But she had no time to dwell on any maternal remorse or the sudden uneasy speculation as to who was responsible for those obvious feminine touches, because a squat, matronly figure was crossing the hall.

Quintina, Mel assumed, which was confirmed as Vann introduced them, speaking to the woman in his fluent Italian.

'Quintina's responsible for making my house a home,' he told Mel, which went some way to explaining the flowers. A surprising degree of relief trickled through her. 'Marco, her husband, tends the gardens and makes sure we all eat healthily. But you won't see him because he's over in Sorrento, so it's just Quintina looking after us today.'

'I have big family. All…' The woman spread her hands. '…i fratelli.' Mel remembered Vann telling her that Quintina had been the fifth of nine siblings, all the rest male. 'I know how to care for…un uomo…man.'

Mel liked her. 'You've had a lot of practice,' she agreed, smiling.

Vann said something to the woman and she laughed. The feeling between them was warm and strong, Mel realised, touched. Some people in Vann's position could so easily have been condescending towards their staff.

'What did she say?' she asked, looking questioningly at Vann after Quintina, still smiling interestedly at her, uttered something rapid in her own language.

Vann said something to his housekeeper which Mel was able to gather was a request for refreshment and which, after expressing her pleasure at meeting Mel, had Quintina scuttling away.

'She said, ''You're very beautiful'',' Vann quoted. '''But be careful. This one has hidden depths''.'

Awkwardly, Mel laughed. 'Is she clairvoyant?' Her voice held a slight tremor.

'I don't know,' he said, and his eyes never left hers. 'Is she?'

The penetration of his gaze caused a tightening in her throat. She wondered if he knew she was lying to him.

Her heart was hammering, but for reasons other than merely being found out as his gaze raked over her hectically flushed cheeks, came to rest on the soft fullness of her parted lips.

'Maybe I'm the one who'll need protection,' he remarked, the suppressed intensity of emotion with which he said it bringing her head up quickly.

For a few moments her eyes searched the cool clarity of his, wide, hungry green pools desperately seeking—yet dreading—recognition. But his lashes came down against her probing scrutiny and his mouth took on a somewhat sardonic twist.

'Let's get to work,' he said.

*   *   *

They spent most of the morning in his study, a room that reflected the tastefulness of the rest of the house with its classic furniture and paintings, its wall to ceiling bookcases and its wide windows, flung open on to the scented garden.

Here, in an oak and glass cabinet near the door, half-obscured by pieces of glassware and ceramics, was a mounted platinum disc. It had caught Mel's unwitting attention almost as soon as she had entered the room.

'My tribute to a spell of madness,' she heard Vann say with a hard edge to his voice, and she swung round, realising he was watching where her interest lay.

Uneasily, she moved away from the cabinet. 'Don't you miss it?' she attempted to say casually, though her tongue seemed to stick to the roof of her mouth.

'No.' His answer was cold and decisive. 'With a management which was rather more light-fingered than tempered and a partnership that was as volatile as the weather, I didn't find too much to commend it.'

He was talking about the arguments within the band that were rumoured, though never fully clarified. And Clayton. Though it had cost thousands to try and retrieve a staggering amount of lost income, it had never been recovered. Clayton had got off through some technical hitch in the law.

'Couldn't that happen in any field of business? Unscrupulous associates? Unsuitable partnerships?'

'Yes,' he accepted. 'Except that the whole experience taught me a hard lesson.'

'Which is?' curiosity made her ask.

'Control and stay in control.'

The harshness of his tone sent an unaccountable little shiver through her. Nevertheless, she felt driven to say, 'I would have thought there was no greater control than having every nubile female in the palm of your hand, having them all screaming for you.'

His face was like a granite mask. 'It palls after a while.'

He meant it, Mel thought. With all that adulation, he had just been doing a job. The leader of a partnership that had let him down in the end, because whatever he had said, he had been the driving force behind it.

'What about you?' With lazy insolence his gaze slid down over her bare shoulders and her breasts beneath the soft sundress, right the way down the length of her golden legs to her pale strappy sandals, and a sardonic smile played around his mouth as he lifted his head again. 'Did I have *you* screaming, Mel?'

His thorough examination had already heightened her senses, but that softly sensual question brought her repressed sexuality fighting for recognition. He meant as Kelly had in innocent hero-worship, but Mel's mind went winging to that raw night in the country hotel. To the blinding, mindless ecstasy of those strong, warm hands on her body, to the moment when he had pushed back the boundaries of her experience and entered her, filling her with his power, each governing thrust rocking her into a different sphere of rapture, a conflagration of need that had torn hard, guttural sobs from the depths of her soul.

She felt the swelling of her breasts and the warm moistness at the very centre of her femininity.

'As you said…' she managed to look at him levelly, hold her voice steady as she advised, ignoring his question '…let's get to work.'

It was nearly lunchtime when Vann announced, 'I need a swim.' Until then they had been discussing his sketches, working towards some innovative ideas for the new campaign. 'Did you bring something to wear? If not, I'm sure I can find a bikini somewhere that might fit you.'

'That won't be necessary,' she said, glad to reject his offer of something that probably belonged to a visiting girlfriend. 'I came prepared.' In fact, she was already wearing her bikini under her sun dress. 'I intended going down to the hotel pool some time this morning. After our meeting,' she added quickly, feeling the need to explain. She didn't want him to think she had been anticipating swimming with him.

'Strapless,' he observed softly when she emerged, a few minutes later, from the luxuriously appointed bedroom where he had said she could undress. Already in the pool, he had swum over to wait for her. On the other side, near the sun loungers, was a water feature of a stone nymph, clothed only in lichen, the water cascading through her slender hands making a silvery sound on the air.

'There's nothing more unsightly than exposing white lines in strapless dresses,' Mel stated rather self-consciously, because he was watching her progress with blatant appreciation, noting unashamedly the movement of her breasts above the brief cups of the apricot bikini, the matching scrap of fabric, fastened with strings, that barely covered the triangle of her sex.

'Yes. I do try to avoid the same problem myself,' he responded, drawing her attention willingly to the sinewy velvet of his shoulders and the deep expanse of that smooth wet chest.

He was all man. But the humour in his face was too much to resist and she started laughing, his remark defusing the situation, helping her to relax.

'If I owned all this,' Mel uttered, stopping, breathless, after covering several laps of the pool, 'nothing could tear me away!' She swam over to sit on the steps just in front of the stone nymph, admiring the luxurious white house with its balconies and bougainvillaea, the backdrop of the mountains, the cloudless blue sky. For the past few years, she remembered someone saying, he'd been living in America. 'I don't know how you can bear to leave.'

'It's the demands of everyday life in the city that make it so much sweeter to return,' he told her, swimming towards her, wet hair gleaming darkly in the sun. 'I spend a lot of my time between New York, Chicago and London, as well as other interesting but hectic capitals. Having been brought up between London and Rome, I feel as though I belong to both countries, but I always come back here when I want to unwind.' He pulled himself up on to the curved marble step beside her, water cascading off him. His thighs, like his upper torso, were powerfully muscled, like every gleaming inch of him, exercised to sinewy athleticism. A line of black hair ran from his navel below that tight waist, drawing Mel's eyes tantalisingly to where it disappeared beneath the band of his dark briefs covering the obvious protrusion of his manhood. She glanced quickly away as he dropped down beside her. 'What about you?'

Wet tendrils framed her face as she met his studied curiosity. 'What about me?'

'Where were you born? Brought up?'

Mel stiffened. She had told him yesterday that she had spent most of her adult life in London. She shrugged. 'We moved around a bit.' Well, that was true, wasn't it? she thought, deliberately avoiding mentioning the Midlands town where she had been living with Kelly. He might remember it from the press reports at the time and start putting two and two together...

He nodded, obviously satisfied, and unconsciously Mel released a deep breath.

'And your parents were divorced.' He was still watching her intently, and Mel bit her top lip. Had she told him that? When he had asked about her family yesterday, she thought, she had simply mentioned that her parents were dead. But she must have...

'Yes. My father left my mother when I was very small— too young to remember much about him.'

'So it's been a case of history repeating itself.'

It took her a moment to grasp what he was saying. Of

course. That her husband had deserted *her* in the same way. She didn't answer, tensing as the wet warmth of his arm casually brushed hers, leaving her stunned by the eroticism of the contact.

'Did you grow up fatherless?' he wanted to know. 'Or did your mother remarry?'

Holding herself rigid, too aware of him, Mel stared down at their legs dangling in the clear water. Hers were golden and smooth against the dark, hair-plastered strength of his.

'She remarried.'

'So at least you had a step-father?'

Mel caught her breath. 'Not for long.' She didn't like these questions, any more than she welcomed this disturbing and dangerous proximity to him, and suddenly she was slipping into the water with the swiftness of an alarmed seal, throwing back curtly over her shoulder, 'He left, too.'

The speed of Vann's reactions startled and surprised her. She hadn't realised he had followed her until she reached the other side. Now, letting her feet touch down, she turned round with a small, shocked gasp as his arms came up on either side of her, entrapping her against the marbled edge.

'Is that why you hate men?' His face was etched with inexorable lines. 'Or was it something else? Something that happened in your own marriage that's made you so over-cautious?'

Mel's breasts rose sharply from her reckless swim across the pool, but also from his threatening nearness that was undermining all her defences, making her snap back, 'I don't hate men.'

She tried to twist away but he wouldn't let her, grasping her chin roughly between a thumb and forefinger.

'Don't you?' he challenged.

'No. That's only some weak excuse you've dreamed up just to salve your own ego.'

'You think my ego needs salving?'

The grim pull of his lips warned her she might be pushing things too far, but she retorted nevertheless, 'Doesn't it?'

'Possibly,' he conceded, 'but I still think you have a problem with men.'

'You would.' She pulled her chin out of his grasp, her features rigid from the shock of his touch. 'Just because I don't want to go to bed with you.'

'Who asked you to?'

Embarrassed heat crept up her throat. She could feel it scorching her cheeks.

'You like making me feel uncomfortable, don't you?' she accused, pressing herself hard against the side for fear of touching him because she was still imprisoned by his arms.

'On the contrary. I'd like to see you relax more, but I don't think you know how because you're afraid.'

'Afraid of what?'

'Commitment. Sex. Rejection. The driving needs of your own body.' He reached for her hand, lifting it from the water. 'This…' Turning the slim appendage, he dipped his head, pressing his mouth to the soft palm, the action so sensual and yet so tender that she found herself battling to contain an emotion that brought tears to her eyes, on top of the devastating sensations already ripping through her body. With mind-blowing sensuality his tongue strayed along her wrist, sending arrows of need piercing through her breasts and loins, keeping her as still as the stone nymph, paralysed from the fear of her own desire. And, as if he knew of her inner fight, he whispered hoarsely, 'I've no intention of doing so, Melissa, but you want me to take you to bed. You want it against all your very practical and rational decisions to the contrary, and that's what you can't—'

A sudden sound pulled them apart. They both looked up, Mel shaken, averting her gaze with embarrassment, Vann appearing no more than mildly irritated by Quintina's coughed intervention. She was saying something Mel had difficulty translating.

'Yes. *Si*, Quintina.' Vann sounded weary, impatient. He said something in Italian.

'*Grazie. Buon giorno*,' she added, addressing Mel.

'*Buon giorno*,' Mel returned, wondering how much the woman had noticed. Still, she was probably used to turning a blind eye to her employer's intimate liaisons with any women he brought here.

'Quintina has an appointment in the village and her taxi has let her down.' Already Vann was springing up out of the pool. 'Stay here and enjoy your swim. I shan't be long.'

He must have dried and dressed himself at lightning speed, because within minutes, stretched out on one of the sun loungers, letting the warm air dry her bikini, she heard the car purr into life on the other side of the house, listening until the note of its engine faded then died away altogether.

Disconcerted by what had happened, Mel turned it over in her mind, wondering how much longer she could keep up this deception. It was driving her crazy, having to be with him without saying anything. And it served her right! she thought. It was just that she would look such an idiot if he found out; no, worse than that. A cheat and a liar. And, despite the little regard he had had for her in the past, might have for her now, what he thought about her mattered. It mattered too much. She just hadn't anticipated the powerful emotional and physical effects he would have upon her. She had been a hapless teenager before, inexperienced in any deeply sexual relationships. She'd been foolish, she had always thought, when she had let her desperate need for him undermine her common sense. When drowning in the sweet oblivion of his caresses and offering pleasure and comfort with her own untutored lovemaking had seemed both natural and right. She was a woman now, she had told herself earlier in the week, and therefore capable of controlling her basic instincts, of keeping things on a strictly businesslike level. But that was before he had touched her. Before she had realised that, despite her thirty-one years and her wider experience of life, she was no more immune to him than she had been nearly fourteen years ago. In fact, his effect on her seemed to have intensified in spite of the years, because no other man had ever made her melt with just one look, with the caress of his voice, with the lift of an eyebrow. No other man had come close to stamping such a lasting mark on her in only a few short hours. And he had the nerve to suggest she had a problem with men!

She was lying face down, trying to steer her thoughts into calmer waters, when her mobile phone started to ring.

Reaching for her canvas bag on the small glass-topped table, Mel delved beneath her purse and a bottle of sunscreen lotion to answer the persistent ringing.

'What is it?' On hearing her daughter's urgent 'Mum?', Mel sat up swiftly, all her protective instincts rushing to the fore. 'Is everything all right?'

'Course, silly,' the young voice responded, unaware of the catastrophes racing through Mel's mind. 'Why wouldn't it be?'

'Because you don't usually ring like this during the day.' They had made an agreement before Zoë left for Rome. 'We said I'd ring you, unless anything happens. Unless it's urgent.'

'It *is* urgent,' Zoë announced rather impatiently. 'I've made a couple of friends. They live in the same apartment block as Karen and Simon. They're going to this pop festival on Friday and they've asked me to go with them. It's just—'

'No!' Mel sprang to her feet to give emphasis to her negation.

'Oh, Mum!'

'No, and definitely *no*!'

'But Mum…'

'No buts, Zoë. I said "no". I'm not having you going to a pop festival on your own.'

'But I won't be on my own. There are four of us going. And Gina's sixteen!'

'I don't care if she's sixty!' Mel could do nothing to temper the panic rising inside her. 'You're not going, and that's final.'

'Why not? Why can't I go?'

'Because I said so.' Roused as Mel was, her own words made her cringe. She had hated anyone saying them to her as a child and couldn't blame her daughter for objecting either as Zoë flung back,

'That isn't good enough! It's because of what happened to Kelly, isn't it?' When Mel didn't answer, sulkily Zoë tagged on, 'Karen said you wouldn't let me go.'

'Well, Karen's right. Put her on.'

'But Mum…!'

'I said, put her on!'

Listening to her daughter muttering something about forgetting what it was like to be young, Mel paced restlessly up and down, waiting for Karen to come on the line.

The high Continental sun was casting dappled rays down through the lance-shaped leaves of an oleander tree behind her, filling the air with the powdery scent of its pink flowers. Beneath her bare feet, the sun-baked terracotta tiles were almost too warm, but she scarcely noticed. Her phone's signal was breaking up and she covered her free ear against the tinkling of the fountain, trying to catch what her friend was saying.

'…when…said…wouldn't want her to…'

'You're darn right I don't! Take her shopping, Karen. Let her go to the zoo. The cinema. Anywhere! But I'm not letting my daughter go to a pop concert. For goodness' sake, Karen! See that she understands. I only—'

The line broke up altogether.

'Hello?' Mel said urgently. 'Hello?' Exasperated, she pressed the redial button, but the display was showing no signal. Letting out a heavy sigh, her features tense with worry, a movement caught her eye and she looked up to see Vann standing on the other side of the pool.

'Trouble?' he enquired crisply.

Taken aback, Mel tried to rearrange her expression into something resembling normality. She hadn't been aware of the car returning. How much had he heard?

'It was just a call from Zoë,' she attempted to explain.

The hard planes and angles of his face, bathed in refracted light from the pool, gave nothing away. 'Nothing wrong, I hope.'

'No. Just the usual headaches from a rebellious adolescent.' She glanced down at her phone, bouncing it agitatedly in her hand. 'Then the signal broke up.' She dropped the phone back into her bag, still open on the lounger.

'Why not use mine?' To her dismay, he was indicating the sitting room beyond the patio doors.

'No, that's all right. I'd finished anyway.'

'It didn't sound like it to me.' Daunting, even in those casual clothes, he was negotiating the pool, moving towards her with a slow, predatory watchfulness. 'It sounded as though you were having the devil's own job getting your point across.'

'Did it?' A nervous little laugh burst from her. She shrugged with an expansive gesture of her hands. 'Well, you know teenagers.' Mistake number one, she realised hopelessly.

His hair, loose now, shone like dark sable as he shook his head. 'I've never had any. But I've been around long enough to realise that at times they can be impossible and that sometimes it might not be easy preventing oneself from overreacting—'

'Overreacting?' Already regretting having made such a scene, her worries over Zoë, coupled with the fear of being found out and now, to crown it all, his criticism of the way she was handling things made her toss back, 'As you've already said, you haven't had any. There's nothing wrong, surely, with a mother being protective of her daughter? Anyway, I hadn't realised anyone was listening.'

'I could hardly help it. You were virtually hysterical,' he said, grimacing, stopping just a metre or so away, hands on hips, legs planted firmly apart. 'But I think we both know why…don't we…*Lissa*?'

CHAPTER SEVEN

SHOCKED, feeling utterly exposed, physically as well as emotionally, standing there in her bikini when he was fully clothed, she stammered, 'How—how did you guess? Was it just now? On the phone?'

He shook his head again. 'I suppose you could say that that just confirmed what I already knew. But I've felt something from the beginning. At the beach. When we met again at the conference. When we were dancing. And yesterday when I saw that photograph of Zoë…'

'Zoë?' Mel enquired, puzzled.

'Yes. She bore an unbelievable likeness to that angry little waif who turned up at my hotel— When was it? Thirteen? Fourteen years ago?'

'Thirteen and a half, to be precise,' she stated pointedly. So that was why his mood had suddenly changed yesterday. 'So why didn't you say something?' she asked half-accusingly.

'Why didn't *I* say something?' he uttered, looking amazed, a broad thumb turned towards his chest. 'You were the one bent on keeping your identity hidden. Why, Lissa? Or is it still Melissa? I'm afraid you'll have to enlighten me, darling. I really can't keep up.' His tone wasn't very gentle, but she supposed she couldn't expect anything else.

'It's Melissa. I just didn't like the name when I was eighteen so I shortened it to Lissa. I wasn't deliberately trying to deceive anybody.' A masculine eyebrow lifted sceptically but, ignoring it, Mel shrugged and said, 'I guess I grew up.'

The gaze that raked over the soft golden swell of her breasts, the flatness of her tummy and the slender legs—

emphasised by the high-cut of her briefs—was obviously assessing that she had—and in more ways than one. His veiled appreciation caused a disconcerting heat to steal through her.

'So why did you lie to me? Pretend you didn't know me?' His features were harsh and censuring against the wild fury of his hair, yet something like mockery touched the firm mouth as he said, 'Embarrassed, Melissa?'

'Can you blame me?' she answered, and only now could she meet his eyes levelly. 'I didn't feel particularly proud of the way I acted that night—sleeping with the man my sister had idolized—and died over because of it.' Particularly when he had never bothered to contact her again.

'But you did it anyway.'

What was he saying? Mel thought, catching the censure in his voice above the breeze that stirred the leaves of the oleander tree. Was it something to do with the note she had sent him afterwards?

'I needed…' *You*, she nearly said, but aloud, rather lamely, substituted, 'someone.' Still she could remember how desperately.

'And I was there.'

'No,' she riposted, defending her actions.

'No,' he accepted quietly, but made it sound like an accusation. 'Tell me the truth, Melissa. Didn't you come looking for me that night with the sole intention of getting me to take you to bed?'

Is that what he believed? 'No!' she stated emphatically again. 'Why would I have done that? I wasn't obsessed with you the way Kelly was. I was grieving—upset, for heaven's sake…!'

Exactly, that same raised eyebrow seemed to be saying. So what was he suggesting? That she should have known better? That they should never have made love at all? Didn't he appreciate the devastating emotions that had driven her into begging him to love her? Hadn't her feelings been apparent when she had sent him that letter? Unless, of course, he had been shocked by what she had written. Or perhaps he hadn't even received it, which would account for why he seemed to be treating her as though making love with him had been some sort of feather in her cap…

'I was angry. I just wanted to talk to you,' she said truthfully.

'But the opportunity presented itself to do a lot more than talk.'

'That isn't how—' she started, but he cut across her protest.

'It was my fault entirely—not yours. I shouldn't have let things get that far. I was older. I could have prevented it. But I was wild and headstrong and you…you were far too…gratifying…to deny.' She had a feeling he was picking his words very carefully. 'So there you have it,' he concluded. 'One ill-timed night of pleasure, instantly regretted by both.'

But I didn't regret it! she wanted to cry out, stung by his casual dismissal of something that had always remained precious to her. *I wrote to you and wanted you to contact me! But you didn't!* Because she had been just a one-night affair for him, she realised achingly now, as she had reluctantly forced herself to accept a long time ago. The only redeeming factor was that because of what he had said about her regretting it, it seemed he had never received that communication from her, and she could only be grateful for that. Perhaps Bern Clayton had never given it to him, she reflected. Or perhaps he had and it had been lost amongst the band's mountains of adoring mail. Or worse, perhaps Vann *had* received it, she thought, considering the possibility as she had done so often in the past, and he had simply chosen to pretend he hadn't, to ignore it.

Still smarting for that wounded eighteen-year-old, too embarrassed to ask, she said carelessly, 'Well, I was young and hurting. And, as you said, you happened to be there. I needed comfort. A diversion. You provided it. That was all.' But her voice cracked with the feelings she was trying to contain, the lie hanging on the silence with the silvery sound of the fountain.

Something drew a fine line between his brows, the only emotion behind an otherwise inscrutable mask. 'No,' he said quietly, moving to breach the gap between them. 'That isn't all.'

Every instinct screamed a warning as he reached out, catching a bright tendril of her hair. 'You'd like me to believe that, but you're only fooling yourself, Melissa. I think, darling,' he breathed, his voice unusually husky, 'that if I touched you I could have you writhing in my arms in exactly the same way as I did before, even though you'd like to convince yourself otherwise.'

Had he noticed the way she was holding her breath? The way the peaks of her breasts had hardened into tight thrusting buds against her insubstantial bikini top?

'Don't, please,' she protested against the hand that was now trailing lightly down the sensitive column of her neck, making her nerve endings shudder with pleasure.

'You implore me, Mel? The cool, self-assured businesswoman? The invincible female? And I thought you were immune.' His face was rigid with an emotion she couldn't define.

'Vann, don't do this,' she pleaded, held captive merely by his nearness. 'We had one night, but that was it. *Finito*.'

'Finito.' His mouth curved faintly, fleetingly. 'Believe me, my love, I haven't even begun with you yet.'

His hand was splayed across the base of her throat, resting lightly across the rapidly pulsing hollow. She swallowed, seeing the need for retribution in those glittering eyes. She had lied, deceived him, just as Bern Clayton had lied and deceived him. He didn't take kindly to being made to look a fool.

'For whatever reason you're trying to deny it, Melissa, you can't prevent this any more than I can,' he rasped, his face going out of focus as he dipped his head, claiming her mouth with his.

Her murmur of protest was lost beneath the hard persuasion of his lips, the hands that had lifted to resist him now trapped against the heated cotton of his T-shirt. The warmth of his arm across her back and the coarse fabric of his chinos against her stomach and bare thighs made her startlingly aware of how little she was wearing. Locked in his arms, she groaned her hopeless need and despair.

'You still deny it?' he challenged, lifting his head after a moment, his breathing harsh and laboured. 'When all I have to do is touch you and you turn to fire.' His lips burned kisses across her cheek, her temple, her hair. 'You're a fraud, Melissa,' he whispered hoarsely. 'And you know what happens to frauds. They get found out.'

He was still angry because she had lied, she thought hectically, that promise of sweet retribution in his voice turning her insides to liquid.

His lips moved down over the perfumed warmth of her throat and shoulders, his hands caressing the sensitive flesh of her upper arms with calculated skill.

Beneath her bikini top her breasts ached for his touch, and she knew an acute need way down inside her as her hips moved sensuously against his, met the hard, unmistakable thrust of his arousal.

Lifting his head, taking a deep breath as though to quell some inner struggle, Vann drew away just enough to unfasten her top and toss it down on to the sun lounger.

His mouth looked vulnerable, she thought, noting absently how his olive skin seemed stretched across the prominent bones of his cheeks as he gazed down on the beauty of her high, rounded breasts. When he looked up, Mel couldn't meet his eyes, knowing her own would betray the longing evoked by his caresses. But, against her will, her engorged breasts were already doing that, and she closed her eyes against the pure pleasure of his hands on their heavy, aching fullness, against his groan of satisfaction, stifling the small sounds he wrung from her as he cupped each creamy mound in turn to suckle their swollen pink aureoles.

She wanted to make love with him. She wanted it as much as she wanted life; to experience the fulfilment she knew now only this man could give her. But she didn't want to offer herself to someone who would use her again just for his own gratification. Wasn't that the word he had used? And yet what he was doing to her was so exquisite. She could feel the warmth of those smooth hands as they slid down over her body, remembering, like it was yesterday, every crease and sinew of their skilled strength, the magic they could work as they moved to massage her hips, then tug at the strings of her briefs.

Under those determined hands, the scrap of material fell away. Mel felt it skim her legs, her last protection, to land with cool disregard at her feet.

She was as naked as a nymph, feeling the warm breeze as a conspirator to arouse her, heightening her pleasure so that she closed her eyes against its sensual caress, against the heat of her own desire and what Vann was doing to her.

His lips and hands were following the same path, down over her breasts and her ribcage, over the smooth plane of her belly, down and down, his body doing their bidding, bending, stooping, kneeling now to cup the pale globes of her buttocks in his hands and taste the sweet nectar of her body.

She gave a throaty, rapturous groan, a nymph glorying in the freedom of her nakedness and the ecstasy of the man who was worshipping her. This man who had brought women to their knees, paying homage to her femininity, drawing, as though from her stone sister beside her, sustenance from the life-spring of her body.

It was exquisite agony. 'No,' she murmured, her head thrown back, praying, yet dreading that he would stop. But his hands on her buttocks tightened to draw her closer, his hair sensually erotic against her heated flesh until all at once she felt the sharp, pleasurable tingling in her thighs. Tension mounted, holding her rigid. She heard her own quickened breathing. Then suddenly with one convulsive sob, she leaned forward to clasp his head, clutching at his thick dark hair as uncontrollable spasms shuddered through her.

As ecstasy receded and normality resumed, she could hear the fountain still trickling beside the pool. The breeze still whispered through the oleander tree, and the sun was beginning to feel like a brand on her bare skin.

Her fingers still clutched the strong, masculine hair, but Vann's cheek lay against the warm plane of her abdomen, his arms tightly clasping her trembling body, giving her time to recover. She felt his lips, feather-light, brush her skin before, eventually, he got to his feet.

'Are you all right?' he enquired hoarsely. He looked flushed and tousled, a sybaritic god, satiated with the pleasure of his goddess.

Mel nodded, unable to speak. Now that it was over, she felt ashamed of her response and acutely self-conscious of her nakedness. She had left her dress in the bedroom. It was only a short step around the pool but it might have been a mile and she didn't think she could stand there and fumble with the strings of her bikini. There was, however, a towel on the sun bed.

Even as the knowledge registered, Vann was peeling off his T-shirt.

'Here,' he said softly. 'Put this on.'

Gratefully, she took it from him. It felt warm and soft and smelled of his musky scent as she pulled it over her head. She was glad it was large. Large enough to be decent, she thought, when it slid over her thighs.

'Quintina prepared some lunch for us before she left. When you're ready,' Vann advised, seemingly unaffected by what had just taken place, 'come and join me in the kitchen.'

He had to be suffering agonies of frustration, Mel thought, watching him walk away, because there was no doubt that he had been as aroused as she was, and she strongly suspected he had sacrificed his own pleasure to prove a point. That she couldn't resist him as a man, whatever the circumstances. That he could drive her wild with her need of him and still remain enough in command of himself to walk away from her afterwards. But why? Why had he been so determined to make her aware of her weakness for him? Was it because she had so rashly stated that making love with him had been no more than a distraction from her grief? Because his ego was so inflated he couldn't bear any woman claiming she was immune to him? Even as she thought it, somehow she didn't think that was true.

And what about her? she asked herself. If she could respond so uninhibitedly to a man who had devastated her life before, against her will, her common sense and her better judgement, had her reasons for making love with him the first time been as excusable as she had always believed? Had it been just sex all along when she had always believed it had been something much more than that? Had she been as besotted with him as the unfortunate Kelly while staunchly refusing to acknowledge it? Was that the subconscious motive, as he had seemed to be suggesting, that had propelled her into seeking him out under the banner of her anger and her misery? To share his bed?

She couldn't even bear to consider that that might be true

of herself and, offering up a silent apology to her sister for her shameful behaviour, she retrieved the scraps of her bikini and retreated to her room where, in the blissful privacy of the *en suite* bathroom, she attempted to scrub away the memory of his touch under the forceful jets of the shower.

They had lunch in the large, country-style kitchen, overlooking Marco's well-tended vegetable garden.

Despite everything, Mel found she was famished and tucked in gratefully to the food Quintina had left them, a simple but satisfying meal of continental cheeses and ciabatta with sun-dried tomatoes, complemented by glasses of the region's cool, clear, white wine.

'I see Harvey was right the other day when he made that rather indelicate remark about your eating habits,' Vann observed wryly, watching with something like approval as she broke off another piece of the crisp and tasty ciabatta. And softly, his words conveying a wealth of meaning, 'Got your appetite back, Mel?'

He was referring, she knew, to what had happened outside, the first time he had made any reference to it. Until then their conversation had been casual, restrained, as though they were both steering away from mentioning it.

She blushed now, bright pink, picking up her glass as a distraction, noticing the mocking twist to his lips, how relaxed he appeared, while she felt stripped of all her defences.

She was pleased when, having stacked the dishwasher to help Quintina, as well as to give herself something to do, they were making their way back to the study. They still had one or two things to sort out for the proposed new campaign.

Coming through the doorway, however, Mel stumbled over her own foot only to find herself caught by a steadying arm.

'Careful,' he warned. 'I don't think Harvey Associates

would look on me too favourably if I were to return its prize executive injured in any way.'

If only you knew! she thought, wondering how she was ever going to recover from today. It had taken her years to get over her experience with him the first time. If she had ever got over it! She had never stopped comparing him with every other man who had come after him. But not this time, she determined, gritting her teeth against his unsettling proximity, because, Heaven help her, her body was responding in the most basic way just from that casual touch.

'Your skin's a bit pink,' he remarked, causing her to stiffen from the light brush of his fingers over her left shoulder. 'We'd better put something on that.'

We?

Swallowing, she said, 'I've got some moisturiser in my bag.'

Quickly she tripped upstairs to the beautifully appointed bedroom where she had changed and showered and applied some of the smooth lotion to the sensitive area. It was a facial moisturiser, but it would have to suffice, she thought. Her back felt sore, too, but she couldn't do anything about that.

'Your back's red,' Vann commented, making her spin round to see him standing in the doorway. 'Are you sure you don't want this?' He was holding up a bottle of *Aprés Sun*.

Oh, hell…. One strap of her dress drawn down, she glanced over her shoulder to inspect herself in the dressing-table mirror.

'Swallow your pride, Mel. Let me.'

Turning round, she stood stock-still as he applied the cool cream to the reddened area, clutching her dress to her bare breasts because he needed to draw both straps down to cream almost down to her bra-line. Her bikini was still hanging over the balcony where she had placed it to finish drying before lunch. She wondered what he would say if he knew she was naked under her dress.

Oh, but his hands were so pleasurable, sliding over her tingling flesh! She closed her eyes against the heightening sensations, against the sight of his dark reflection in the mirror and all that he was doing to her. Desire tautened her bare nipples, sent a hard contraction spearing through her lower body. He had given her fulfilment in the most intimate way and yet it wasn't enough…

'I know. It's agony, isn't it?' he said huskily, shocking her eyes open to meet the tense need in his reflected features, the raw hunger in hers. Dear heaven! How could it have betrayed her? She looked wanton, wild and wet. 'I've been thoroughly guilty of self-deception,' he rasped, his hands clamping on to her upper arms. 'Any man who makes love to you and says he regrets it is a liar. I didn't regret it.' He swore almost viciously and spun her round to face him. 'I wanted you then as much as I want you now. I can't fight it any longer. I'm as worked up as you are, Mel.'

When his mouth descended on hers she was already dragging him down to her, taking as much as he was, her hands and mouth as greedy and devouring as his. It was as if a pressure valve had just exploded, a burst of boiling emotions that had no choice but to be released.

All restraint gone now, he was tugging at her dress, ripping it down while she grasped wildly at the clean T-shirt he had donned, pulling it out of the waistband of his trousers.

'God, Mel…'

He lifted her effortlessly off her feet as he had done the first time, and carried her over to the king-sized bed, coming down beside her and taking over her attempt to divest him of his clothes.

He was so wonderfully male, from the contoured muscles

of his hair-furred limbs and torso to the prominent symbol of his sex.

She was still wet from his earlier kisses, and even that was a turn on, her legs spreading like a butterfly's wings, inviting him, ready for him as he sheathed himself with a condom from the bedside cabinet and took her without the need for any foreplay, plunging deep into the cushioning warmth of her body.

'You're beautiful,' he whispered much later. 'And you make love beautifully. Just as I remember. Even at eighteen—hating me as you did—you were everything a man could wish for in his bed.'

She was lying on her side, her head on his shoulder, one arm flung carelessly across him. The bedroom door was still open, and she wondered what Quintina would say if she came back and found them.

I didn't hate you, she wanted to respond, but didn't. Instead, finding her voice, she murmured, 'That's praise indeed, coming from a man who must have had scores of women.'

'Hardly scores.'

'You had them throwing themselves at you.' And probably still do, she thought with a startling degree of jealousy. 'Night after night.'

He made a wry sound down his nostrils. 'I must admit the opportunities were there.'

'But you resisted them all like the Sir Galahad you were.'

'Not all, Mel,' he murmured softly, his arm tightening around her. 'I didn't resist you, did I?'

But he'd intended to, she thought. Even then, young as he was, he'd shown restraint at first when she'd been initiating the moves, when she had begged him not to leave her, but thankfully he wasn't reminding her of that.

'As I said, you made quite an impression. Your siren's

cries as I made love to you haunted me for a long time afterwards.'

So she hadn't been cast out of his thoughts quite as quickly as she had imagined. The knowledge gave rise to a crazy leap of hope.

'But you didn't do anything about it.' Even if he hadn't got her letter he could have found a way to contact her if he'd wanted to, she thought. Even Bern Clayton had assured her of that.

'Well, no,' Vann conceded, as though she shouldn't have expected anything else. 'I didn't actually think it was wise in the circumstances.'

Because of Kelly? Or because, having thought about it afterwards, he could see no future in any relationship between them?

Hope faded, leaving only the warm, moist lethargy of their lovemaking.

'No,' she breathed tightly, so he wouldn't know how much she had wanted him to. Yet when he turned round, rolling on top of her, she winced from the sheer pleasure of his warm, heavy body on hers.

His lips were nipping the sensitive flesh at the juncture of her neck and shoulder. Even the brush of his hair against her jaw was an unbearable turn on. She wanted him again like she had never wanted anyone. Yet all her instincts of self-preservation told her she was going to get hurt.

Those warm, slightly rough hands had already recommenced their treacherous magic, shaping the soft contours of her body. She sucked in her breath, her senses swimming from the moist heat of his tongue over her nipple, from the heady musk of their bodies, so that it took every ounce of her will to summon up the strength to say, 'Vann... Vann, I don't want an involvement.'

He inhaled sharply, and the lips that were performing their sweet torture stilled against her breast. After a moment he lifted his head to look at her. Her eyelids were heavy, her cheeks flushed with desire and her flaming hair, damp at the temples, lay tousled across his pillow.

'My dear girl, if you hadn't noticed, we *are* involved,' he murmured, a sensual smile touching his mouth, though his features were gripped by the same depth of wanting that enslaved her. 'I'm not a fatalist, but there are some things that happen just because they're meant to. This…chemistry, as you called it, has been there between us from the beginning. Even before you collapsed, sobbing and helpless in my arms. Oh, yes,' he said heavily when she looked amazed by his declaration. 'I'd never seen a girl with so much courage and spirit as I thought you had that night. I saw you and I wanted you.'

But not enough to make you want to find me again, she thought achingly.

When she didn't answer, afraid that she might say too much, he repeated, 'We are involved, Mel, for what it's worth. Deceiving yourself won't change that—won't alter the fact that you want me as much as I want you. So let's enjoy what we have. Here and now. I'm not asking for commitment.'

No, of course not, and she should be grateful that he was being honest, she thought, wanting him too much to think beyond the pleasure her murmur of acceptance would guarantee her.

Too weak to deny herself, as once again his seeking mouth found her breast, she clasped him to her with a small moan of defeat, giving herself up to the driving needs of her sexuality.

Over the next few days they saw each other every second they could spare, making love at whatever moments they could steal. At the villa. In her room. On his yacht, moored in a small, private cove, under the stars. They couldn't get enough of each other, sometimes ripping one another's clothes off as soon as they found themselves alone, a slow, leisurely ecstasy always following their first, urgent coming together.

'I never realised it could be like this,' Mel said, after one particularly adventurous session of lovemaking. 'I used to wonder why some people made so much fuss about sex.'

'Sex?' Vann queried, as though he thought the word too mild to describe their torrid, almost desperate need for each other's bodies. Then, after a moment, 'It's just as well it wasn't Harvey you decided to seduce on this trip. Somehow I don't think he would have quite come up to matching that passionate nature of yours.'

They were on Vann's yacht, having sailed around the coast that morning. It was their last day together. Now, sunbathing on deck, naked and feeling slightly bruised in places from that passion he had spoken of, listening to the waves lapping gently against the hull, she thought of what Jonathan had said to her two days before.

'You're sleeping with him, aren't you?' And when she had thrust her chin up, refusing to discuss what was, after all, none of his business, 'You must be mad!' he had thrown at her. 'You aren't kidding yourself there's any future in it, are you?'

She wasn't but she'd hated hearing Jonathan remind her of the fact, especially when he had gone on, 'He's a world-renowned entrepreneur and a multi-millionaire, for heaven's sake! People like him move in different circles from the likes of you and me. He's just having a fling with someone who's willing. I just hope you know what you're doing,' he had added condescendingly.

She did, because Vann had told her nothing but the truth. He wasn't looking for commitment. Not with her, anyway. And, as far as knowing what she was doing was concerned, well, she did, didn't she? When this week was through she would leave here, fly to Rome, and spend the following week touring Tuscany with Zoë. Bed and breakfasting. Taking it as it came. It had sounded like fun when they had planned it. And it would be, Mel determined, for Zoë's sake. After which, she would return to her normal, everyday life and pretend this madness had never happened. That this crazy affair she was conducting with Vann was enough to sustain her through her loveless existence. That she had never been in danger of actually falling in love with him…

'Do you have to go to Tuscany?' he was enquiring, as though reading her thoughts.

Lying face down on a towel, she lifted her head to look at him. He was as naked as she was, lying on his back beside her.

'Spend your extra week here. With me,' he startled her by saying.

At his villa? 'I can't…' Her throat felt dry and her heart was beating crazily. 'I've made arrangements.'

'Break them.'

'Besides, I'll have Zoë.'

'So…' He rolled over on to his side, his big body gleaming, head supported by an elbow. 'I like children. Another week together, Mel. Think of it.'

And have longer to increase the agony of parting from him?

She turned round to face him, adopting the same position. Her breasts hung tantalisingly and she felt his gaze drop to their pink buds, still erect from his kisses, incredibly sensitive.

'It wouldn't be the same,' she felt she needed to tell him, fighting the strongest desire to accept. Even as he lay, relaxed, stretched out beside her, she could see what she was doing to him. She had to stem the urge to reach for him…

'No. I appreciate that we will have to…' he lifted a hand to trace the tempting valley between her breasts '…temper our behaviour somewhat.' Even that light touch was stimulating.

'And after that?' she tried to say nonchalantly.

He seemed to hesitate before answering. 'I told you. No strings. That was what we agreed, wasn't it?'

Of course. She hoped the sudden sharp anguish inside her didn't show. 'It really isn't such a good idea.'

'Thanks, but no thanks?' His tone was surprisingly bitter. 'So what's there left to say? Have a good trip? It's been fun knowing you?' There was an almost fatalistic air about the way he said it, as though he had accepted it was pointless pursuing the relationship. She should have been glad, but her heart felt as if it were being ripped out of her.

'I've got other commitments, Vann. Bookings. Plans. I can't renege on those.'

'Of course not.' His eyes were hard, his mouth suddenly grim. 'Ever the hard-headed, self-sufficient female.'

'That's not fair!'

'Do you have any dreams, Melissa?' She wondered why he sounded so angry. 'Have you ever had a dream?'

'Yes.' She sat up, looking over his shoulder. In the distance, the dark bulk of Nureyev's island slumbered in the afternoon heat. 'I wanted that self-reliance that you're so keen to poke fun at. I wanted to be my own person and be totally successful at what I did.' And I wanted a real home, with a brother or sister for Zoë and a man to love me. But she didn't say that, uttering a small cry of protest as he suddenly reached for her, pulling her on top of him to roll her beneath him, pinning her there with his wrists and his arousing weight.

'Well, you've achieved your objective, darling, because you're definitely your own person and you're certainly successful at this!'

He kissed her then, hard and punitively, as he had kissed her in Amalfi, only this time Mel responded with a desperate anger of her own. She wanted to hurt him, as much as she was hurting inside, for his not loving her when he had made her love him, because she had to acknowledge now that she was in love with him. She always had been. He had stolen her heart that night in the country manor, which was why she had never been able to respond in quite the same way to anyone else since.

They made love like it was the last time. Because it was the last time, she thought. And if she kept telling herself she was being crazy refusing to stay, then she had to keep reminding herself that if she had accepted his offer, not only would she have become more deeply involved with him, but it would have laid her open to further, more complicated issues that she didn't want to face.

CHAPTER EIGHT

NAPLES Airport was busy, with mainly tourists making up the long queues to the check-in desks.

Battling through the crowd, Mel had a job finding the appropriate check-in point for her internal flight. Her suitcase was unwieldy, even on its castors, and the strap of her flight bag was cutting into her shoulder. After a virtually sleepless night, she wasn't feeling her best. She missed the others, too. The rest of her team had flown home yesterday, and this morning the last cases for the remaining clients had stood waiting with hers in the hotel lobby. Then they had gone, and she had been the last to depart.

The conference room had lain silent when she had checked it for the last time, the empty tables and chairs seeming to accentuate her sudden crushing isolation. Ever since she had left England she had had company. First Zoë and Karen, then Jonathan and the team, and Vann.

Vann. She tried not to think about him and the miles she had already put between them—the knowledge that she could still have been with him—as she paused for a moment amidst the maddening chaos to get her bearings, decide where she had to go.

Jostled uncomfortably by someone rushing past, she adjusted the strap that had almost been knocked off her shoulder and, seeing the sign for her airline, fought her way through a sea of bodies to join the queue for Rome.

Everyone seemed to be with someone, she noticed, having nothing better to do than scan the endless queues as she waited in line. Families with children. Couples.

She seemed to be the only one on her own, she thought

with such a strong wave of loneliness sweeping over her it had her staring down at her suitcase in an attempt to blot out the scene.

She had Zoë, didn't she? And she wasn't so much alone as footloose and fancy free. It was just this place—the crowds—that was making her feel lonely. Plus the fact that she had been with so many other people this week.

'Tickets, please.'

Relieved to see that she was next in line, Mel reached for the zipper on the side compartment of her flight bag. It was gaping open. She must have forgotten to close it when she had tipped the taxi-driver, she thought hectically, although she knew she hadn't.

Frantically, she rifled through what remained of the contents she had checked and double-checked before leaving the hotel. It wasn't possible, she thought, unable at first to comprehend the truth. But then the realisation hit her like a punch in the ribs, and to no one in particular she was exclaiming, 'My passport! My purse! Everything! It's gone!'

The check-in staff obviously weren't very impressed.

'I had everything when I came in. I know I did,' Mel stated emphatically to the exasperated-looking young Italian woman and her older male counterpart who had been summoned to help sort out what should be done.

She would have to tell the police. Get a statement from them to help with her emergency passport. Contact the British Consulate.

But all that was going to take time.

'I have to ring my daughter,' Mel told him urgently. 'I'm meeting her in Rome.' Karen and her husband were flying off to Switzerland to celebrate their second wedding anniversary as soon as Mel arrived. She had arranged to meet them all at the airport, and now there was no way she would be able to make it on time.

ELIZABETH POWER   133

She reached for her mobile phone in the same compartment where her purse and document wallet had been, her
arm drooping uselessly on realising that the thief had taken
that as well.

'Do you have a phone I can use?' she requested, trying
to remain calm. 'I've got to contact my friend.'

In the small inner office to which she was taken, however,
another realisation struck Mel. She had had Karen's mobile
number on a piece of paper tucked into her purse. But now
her purse was gone, along with all her money, her travellers'
cheques and her credit cards. As the scale of her predica-
ment hit her, Mel found it hard even to think.

She'd have to cancel her cards, she pulled herself together
sufficiently enough to realise. But the twenty-four hour
emergency number had been keyed into her mobile phone
book—and the thief had that! A bubble of hysterical laughter clogged her throat from the irony of it all. After a great
deal of effort, however, she managed to make the man beside her understand what she wanted and, with his help,
succeeded in cancelling her cards.

Next, apologising profusely to him, she quickly tapped
out the number of Zoë's mobile phone, only to be told it
was switched off.

Probably she had used up her credit limit—or forgotten
to charge her battery, Mel thought, exasperated. But if she
couldn't telephone Karen or Zoë, how was she going to let
them know she wouldn't be arriving as planned? They
would already have left the house, Mel realised with a swift
glance at her watch, and Simon's studio would be closed
now for the weekend, so there would be no chance of catching anyone there who could give her Karen's number. She
was stranded here with no one to contact, no money, and
therefore no hope of reaching her daughter—and that was
the only thing that mattered. She didn't even care that the

rest of their holiday would probably now have to be cancelled. She had to get to Zoë. But how?

Racked with worry, she dropped the phone on to its rest, her face telling its own tale. 'What am I going to do?' she asked, harrowed.

The man gave a sympathetic shrug. 'There is no one…?'

Battling against the thought that had just come into her mind, Mel shook her head. But the thought grew and flourished, goading and tormenting her. Well, there wasn't anyone else, was there?

Grabbing the phone again, Mel managed to reach the operator and waited, her heart in her mouth, for the connection to be made.

'*Buon giorno*,' Quintina answered when Mel was put through.

'It's Mel, Quintina. Mel Sheraton. Is Vann there?' He isn't, she thought desperately, following a sudden silence when she thought she had been cut off.

'Melissa?' Relief closed Mel's eyes as the deep voice came over the line, curious, strung with surprise.

'Oh, Vann! I need your help. It's Zoë.'

'Zoë?' Surprise gave way to concern. 'What's happened to her?'

'Nothing,' Mel quickly assured him. 'But I can't get to her. She'll be waiting in Rome and I've missed my flight because I've been robbed! They've taken everything!'

'Whoa! Whoa! Take it easy.' Through the loud announcement of a plane being ready to board and the sudden rush of activity in the passenger terminal outside, Vann's voice was soothing and calm. 'Now, tell me again, slowly.'

So she did, and when she had finished he said without any further ado, 'Stay exactly where you are. I'm coming to get you.'

'But what about Zoë? She'll be waiting at the airport. Karen and Simon will have to cancel their trip because of me. And I've imposed upon them enough. I don't think they'll leave her, but she might try and persuade them to. She's so strong-willed and determined. I'll never forgive myself if anything happens to her.'

'Nothing's going to happen to her,' he stressed phlegmatically, taking control. 'I've got contacts in Rome. I'll send a car for her and leave a message at Arrivals in case you can't contact her before she gets there. Don't worry. Everything's going to be all right.'

Mel's lashes came down as she took a deep breath to steady herself. He was right. Of course he was. 'I don't want to put you to all this trouble,' she said apologetically. 'Just as long as Zoë's all right. You don't have to worry about me.'

An almost amused chuckle came over the line. 'And why would I worry about Zoë and then leave her mother stranded at Naples Airport?'

Because she's young and vulnerable. Because she's only twelve. *And because she's your daughter, too!*

For a moment Mel thought she had screamed it aloud. It was only when Vann said calmly, 'Do as you're told. I'm coming to get you,' that she realised she hadn't.

He was with her in such a relatively short time that Mel didn't dwell on how fast he must have driven to cut the nearly two-hour journey by as much as he had. But waiting in the airport lounge, having been interviewed by police and kept supplied with coffee by a generous member of staff, Mel felt herself weakening with joy as she saw him striding towards her.

'Vann.' The next moment she was being embraced by his warm strength, her arms around him, her head against the coarse fabric of his shirt. 'Thank you for coming.' It seemed an inadequate thing to whisper, especially after the way she had shunned his suggestion of spending her holiday with him.

'My pleasure,' he whispered hoarsely. 'What are friends for?'

Crazily, that simple remark brought tears to her eyes. She hadn't realised he'd ever consider her a friend.

It was a relaxed, easy journey back to the villa. Sitting there, between the jagged coast and the towering reaches of the mountains, Mel thought how all the gods had to be working for Vann because he had got his own way, hadn't he? He hadn't wanted her to leave. And fate, it seemed, had stepped in to help him.

'It seems to be becoming a habit—rescuing Sheraton women,' he commented dryly, unaware of how that simple remark touched something deep down in Mel.

Because, of course, he had saved Zoë's life that day without even realising he was already responsible for that life...

Through suddenly blurred vision, she looked at him steering the car with his usual competence, a glance at his dark profile making her whole being ache with the need to tell him. But all she said lightly, with her eyes guarded, was, 'You must be feeling pretty smug.'

Flicking a switch to block out the fumes from an ancient truck they were following, he said, glancing in her direction, 'Why should I feel smug? In a minute you'll be saying I engineered the whole thing just to bring you back here. I might have, if I'd thought of it,' he added rather dryly, 'but I didn't. You've suffered a trauma,' he went on. 'You've lost all your valuables and you've been at your wits' end over Zoë. Of course I don't feel smug. Oh, I admit I'm glad you're still here. And I'd be lying to say that I wasn't more than happy to be taking you home with me. But smug I definitely am not!'

So that was her suitably chastened, Mel thought, grateful, in spite of what he had said, that he had taken control. Grateful, too, for the message he had left at Rome Airport for Karen to ring him on his mobile, for getting Karen to contact her while she had been waiting at Naples. She had even managed to speak to Zoë.

Now, sitting beside the man she loved, with Zoë on her way to join them, Mel tried not to dwell on the inevitable complications that lay ahead.

'I can't get over this place!' Zoë enthused, coming down the villa's sweeping staircase.

She had been expressing as much ever since she had arrived, with far more bags than she had left with, bursting with excitement about the drive down from Rome, the humorous Italian chauffeur who had teased and joked with her for most of the journey, the stupendous car.

'It even had a video screen fitted into the back of the seat in front and a whole load of videos!'

If Mel had been concerned about her daughter being bored on such a long drive alone then she needn't have been, she'd thought wryly, remembering to thank Vann later for selecting that particular car and driver.

'Did you think I'd forgotten what it was like to be young?' he had said with a crooked smile, pulling her against him as she got up from one of the deeply cushioned sofas to go to bed. She had left Zoë luxuriating in bubbles in her own personal *en suite* bathroom earlier, singing her head off. Quintina and Marco had already retired to their private rooms. 'I might not have kids of my own, but I am aware that their boredom threshold can sometimes use a little bolstering. And I think the least you can do is thank me properly.'

Before she had known what was happening, he had covered her mouth with his, evoking a wild response from her with his hard virility. She had moaned against his mouth, ignoring the goading little voice inside her that screamed she should be telling him the truth, not leading him on like this without his knowing the facts. And she would, she told herself, but not now. Not yet.

But he hadn't let their hunger for each other get out of hand, exercising immense self-control, although he was flushed and breathing heavily as he lifted his head.

'I promised you restraint,' he said, which he had, on the journey down. 'So I think you'd better go to bed before I completely abandon that promise and take you here and now.'

If only you would, she had thought, remembering he had insisted on separate bedrooms as well. She thought it was because of Zoë, but then couldn't help the nagging suspicion that it might be because of his staff. The previous week he had been discretion itself, only making love with her at the villa if no one else was around. But if the two of them shared a room, leaving no doubt in anyone's mind that they were lovers, perhaps he was worried that the relationship might become public…

Frustrated, troubled by doubts and her own conscience, she had fled.

That had been two days ago and now, in the brightness of the sunny morning, Mel tried to shake off her worries, share some of Zoë's delight in her surroundings and this unexpected turn of events that had meant discarding their original plans and coming here instead. But she couldn't. Now that Zoë was here there was every chance that the child might say something to Vann that would make him realise her mother hadn't been straight with him. Not that she had actually lied, Mel deliberated, thinking back. Just that she hadn't actually corrected him when he'd made such blatantly inaccurate assumptions. She had let him go on believing something that wasn't true, and now there was no easy solution to putting things right. Anyway, what was she supposed to do? Come right out and say it?

Oh, by the way, she's your daughter. Mel caught her

breath from just thinking about what his reaction might be, and felt that gnawing anxiety that always surfaced every time she thought about telling him.

'I'm going for a swim,' Zoë announced, stepping lithely off the bottom stair. She had tied a large coloured scarf, sarong-style, around her small, developing figure. 'Vann said he'd help me with my butterfly stroke. Are you coming, too?'

Through the archway, beyond the sitting room and the open patio doors, the pool looked temptingly blue and still.

Mel shook her head. 'No. You run along,' she advised. All her tensions over being robbed, coupled with finding herself in this situation which she had been so keen to avoid, seemed to have come to the fore this morning, causing the familiar dull pain above one eye. Besides, just thinking about the shocking intimacy she and Vann had shared by the pool on that first occasion only made her blush to her roots and her temple throb. 'I've got a threatening headache,' she enlarged.

Zoë's nose wrinkled as she groaned a protest. 'You always say that when you want to get out of doing something.'

'I do not!' Mel replied a little too sharply. She knew she had misled Vann, but she certainly wasn't guilty of ever lying to her daughter. 'That's unfair and you know it is.'

'And what are you accusing your mother of trying to get out of?'

They both looked up as Vann came down the stairs, wearing dark swimming shorts, a blue towel slung over one shoulder. His body was beautiful, lean and tanned and fit, and Mel was startled to realise how much her fingers ached to touch him.

'Having a swim with us,' Zoë told him, looking rather sheepish suddenly. 'She says she's got a headache.'

'Then you must accept what she says.' Those blue eyes

clashing with Mel's made her pulse beat ridiculously fast. 'I think she deserves an apology, don't you?'

Zoë looked shocked at what he was suggesting. His gaze, however, was fixed so penetratingly on her that the girl backed down, looking at her sandalled feet as she murmured, 'Sorry, Mum.'

Over her head, Mel and Vann exchanged glances. 'Run along,' he said to Zoë. 'I'll join you in a minute.' Not needing to be told twice, the child obeyed, her eager footsteps echoing over the marbled tiles.

'A bit of air and relaxation might do your headache some good,' he suggested softly, with a look that said he knew why she was so reluctant to join them outside. Perhaps that was why he was so insistent on keeping their affair under wraps, she thought suddenly. Simply for her sake, although she doubted it. She hadn't realised, though, that being without a man for so long had made her so shy. 'How about it, Mel?'

Why did she find it so easy to be persuaded by him? she wondered when, having substituted her apricot bikini for her shorts and sun top, she was floating on the blue water some minutes later. But he was right. Her headache had eased, she realised, listening to her daughter's giggling attempts to follow Vann's patient instructions, her ears attuned to his deep, companionable laughter, his every casual word, the sheer addiction to his nearness driving any other unwanted thoughts from her mind.

Lying, face upturned to the sun, using only the gentlest movement of her hands and feet to keep her buoyant, Mel thought how great he was with Zoë. He had taken them both water-skiing the previous day, and then during the afternoon had arranged a trip for the child with the gentle, moustached Marco and his ten-year-old grandson to a local farm where they were both able to ride.

As far as her own problems went, he had been helpful in

the extreme. She marvelled at the dexterity and speed with which he had helped sort things out for her—transfers of money, getting her new passport processed, translating in his fluent Italian where necessary.

'Watch that beautiful skin,' he whispered, his head suddenly coming up out of the water right beside her. 'Or I shall be left with the not altogether punishing task of having to rub sun cream all over you, and you know what happened last time.'

A lick of desire passed through her, so intense she lost her balance and would have gone underwater if he hadn't caught her. But the brush of his flesh against hers was too erotic for comfort, especially after their sustained abstinence, and with a sudden wrench she was striking out for the edge of the pool, his laughter following her with the tinkling sound of the fountain.

Zoë pulled a knowing face as she swam up alongside Mel.

'Just think. If you married *him*—he'd be my dad,' she breathed, clearly relishing the idea, but Mel's insides knotted up.

She'd have to tell her—tell them both, she thought but weighed down by her anxieties all she could manage at that moment was, 'Just think again.'

A sudden splash made them turn. Vann had swum right up behind them.

'You heard her, Zoë.' He was reaching for the edge, hauling himself up out of the water. 'There's definitely no chance that your mother and I will ever be getting married.'

Heart sinking, Mel watched him stoop to grab his towel from one of the loungers and stride off across the patio into the house.

Had he heard her? Was that why he had said that? she wondered, mortified. Or was he simply making it clear to *her* that their relationship was definitely a no-strings attached affair? Convinced of the latter, she turned and plunged forcibly under the blue water, striking out against the screaming anguish in her heart.

The following day, Vann drove Quintina into Positano to do some shopping, and Zoë leapt at the chance to go with her when Quintina suggested it.

It was agreed that Marco would pick them up on his way back from a neighbouring vineyard later in the morning, which meant that Vann would be free to return to the villa as soon as his own business was done.

Mel's heart leapt like a gazelle when she heard him discussing the arrangements with them in their own language and grasped that, with Marco gone as well, she and Vann were going to be entirely alone.

Minutes later, seeing them off, watching Vann's indulgence with Zoë, noticing the way he teased her, ruffling her hair as she tripped, giggling, ahead of him out of the villa, made Mel's heart contract painfully.

They should *know*, she thought. And promised herself again that she would tell them…soon. She just hoped Zoë didn't say anything that might start Vann thinking. It was a risk she took every time the two of them were together, she thought, which meant her nerves were strained to breaking point for a lot of the time. Still, Zoë was going to be with Quintina for most of the morning, and Vann was coming back on his own. His departing, 'I'll be back shortly,' caused her insides to quiver with traitorous anticipation, making her wonder if she had imagined that meaningful glitter in his eyes.

Aching for nothing now but his return, Mel raced upstairs, changing the shorts and T-shirt she had pulled on after she had showered for the floaty, feminine skirt she had purchased the previous week. The flame and ochre colours reflected the highlights in her loose and riotous hair, she noted, teaming it with a plunging V-necked lemon top which, as she was braless, showed off the tantalising fullness of her breasts. Low, strappy gold sandals accentuated her tanned feet. Some mascara, a little lipstick, and a spray of perfume. There, she thought, catching sight of her flushed features and her wide, dilated pupils in the mirror. She looked like a sex slave, eagerly awaiting initiation by her master.

She gasped as the phone rang, like some criminal caught in the act of doing something she shouldn't.

It was the police in Naples. Amazingly, they had found her passport and her purse, emptied save for a book of stamps and a photograph. The man spoke good English and said she could collect them on production of some identification.

'Thanks,' she uttered breathlessly, ringing off.

She should start packing, she chided herself, hearing Marco's car start up outside. Not titivating herself to try and seduce a man who didn't really want her. Because that was all she was doing, she realised.

Five minutes after the sound of Marco's car died away she heard the low growl of Vann's, and reached the foot of the stairs just as he was mounting the steps. The front door was open, spilling sunlight into the wide hall with the lucid note of a bird on the scented air. But Mel was senseless to everything but the man.

In a long-sleeved white shirt and dark trousers, he was looking down at the steps and didn't see her at first, and her heart gave a painful lurch.

He'd want to make love to her. He had to want it as much as she did, she thought desperately, feeling every feminine cell leap towards his hard masculinity.

Then, as he came in, he looked up and saw her, and the blood suddenly drained from her face.

'What's wrong? What is it?' she murmured. His face, too, seemed bloodless, and there was a cold severity to his mouth that almost frightened her.

'Well, well,' he said, shutting out the scented garden with one forceful thrust of his hand. 'Are you wearing anything under that, Mel? Or do I have to wait until I rip it off you to find out?'

'Vann…' What is it? she had been going to ask, but that hard edge to his voice stopped her.

'Isn't that what you want me to do, Mel?'

'No…' She did, but she couldn't understand why he was being like this.

'Oh yes, Melissa, I think it is.' He was moving in that dark predatory way of his towards her, and unconsciously she grabbed the carved newel post just behind her for support. 'But then you've always found difficulty telling the truth, haven't you?'

Oh *no*!

'Oh yes,' he breathed again, seeing her dismay. 'Fortunately, Zoë doesn't seem to have followed in the same footsteps as her mother.'

Mel didn't need to ask him what he meant. So this was it, she thought, what she had dreaded all along, and steeled herself for his tirade, his inevitable anger.

'There's a whole year's difference between only just twelve and thirteen in two weeks!' he tossed at her. 'I wouldn't have known if I hadn't heard her innocently telling Quintina. That means she was born around seven months after we…' He broke off, looking wounded, baffled, as though he were trying to comprehend. 'Unless you were already pregnant when we made love that night…' His breath seemed to shudder through the hard cavity of his chest. 'She's mine, isn't she?' His hands were on her shoulders, hard against her smooth skin. 'Isn't she?' he demanded heavily.

Mel's Adam's apple worked nervously, an irrational fear gripping her. She could have denied it, told him she had already been pregnant, as he had just so lightly suggested.

At least that could have excused her so carelessly having sex with him without any precautions. But there had been enough deception, she thought, and with a small sigh of defeat, shoulders slumping, she said, 'I was going to tell you, but the time just never seemed right. She was born two months premature, and I nearly lost her. It was touch and go—whether she'd survive—all the way through.' The doctors had said it was because of losing Kelly and her mother so close together, but that fact alone made her baby the only thing to hang on to—made Zoë all the more precious to her when she had survived.

'Why didn't you tell me? Straight away? As soon as you found out?' He was shaking his head, still trying to understand.

'I didn't think you'd want to know. Especially as I'd already written.'

'Yes, well…'

He wasn't questioning that? Did that mean he'd received her letter?

'You got my note?' she uttered incredulously.

'Yes,' he said grimly, his hands falling away from her. So why did he look—sound—so forbidding? 'You really didn't believe in holding anything back, did you?'

His words cut her to the quick. She'd always known she'd been a fool to write it. A total fool, she thought achingly as, angry and clearly upset at having been denied his parental right, he roughly went on, 'What did you decide when you found out you were pregnant? That you'd burnt all your bridges? Or wouldn't your pride let you contact me?'

Because he hadn't replied?

'You missed your chance there, Melissa.' His laugh was harsh and mirthless. 'You could have whacked a nice fat paternity suit on me!'

Her eyes were dark with bewilderment. 'Why would I have wanted to have done that?' And, when he didn't answer, 'Did you think I was just after your money?' she whispered, having never considered that possibility.

Letting out a huge sigh, rather wearily he said, 'No,' shaking his head. 'However else I reacted at the time, I didn't seriously think there'd be any more repercussions from tumbling into bed with Lissa Ratcliffe. I knew you weren't a gold-digger.'

Well, thank heaven for that! Mel thought, stung nevertheless by the way he had referred to their lovemaking.

'Sheraton,' she said then, coming clean.

He frowned. 'What?'

'Kelly and I had different fathers. Kelly's name was Ratcliffe. Mine was Sheraton.'

A host of conflicting emotions chased across his face. 'So...there wasn't any husband, either?'

Contritely, she shook her head.

'Yet you let me think there was. Lied to me. About everything,' he said hoarsely. 'About who you were. About Zoë.' Anger surfaced, darkening those glittering irises. 'About her age.'

'No!' He was looking at her as though he didn't know who she was any more and she couldn't bear it. She hadn't wilfully set out to deceive anyone, beyond keeping him from guessing who she was, and only then because she was so embarrassed at meeting him again. 'OK, I lied about having met you before,' she admitted with heartfelt remorse, 'but I felt so dreadful.' How was I supposed to feel? she thought. I sent you a letter but you hadn't bothered to reply. Not that I ever really expected you would, but I wanted you to. So much! 'But I didn't blatantly lie about anything else. When you asked how old Zoë was and I said...' She thought back, trying to remember. 'I don't know exactly what I said, but I only meant she wouldn't be twelve for much longer, but you assumed the opposite. You assumed everything! I didn't actually tell you I'd been married. You assumed it.

Just like you assumed everything else. It was what you wanted to believe!'

'And you let me. Misled me all the way through. Even about my own daughter.' Bare emotion slashed harsh lines across his face. 'Didn't you think I had a right to know?' She glanced away, looked down at his dark slip-on shoes, unable to bear the tortured accusation in his eyes. He grasped her roughly, forcing her to face him. 'Didn't you think Zoë had a right to know?'

'Stop it!' He had hurt her where it hurt most, at the very core of her maternal pride, and she tried to pull away, but he wouldn't let her, his fingers bruising the tender flesh of her upper arms.

'What do you say to her, Mel? What do you tell her when she asks? That you don't know who her father is? Or do you spin her some cock-and-bull story to try and deceive her, too?'

'No!' Now her own anger gave her the strength to twist out of his grasp. 'I've never deceived her! How dare you even accuse me of doing that? If you must know, she knows her father was someone I met very briefly, even if she doesn't know the circumstances, or exactly who you are. But I've always told Zoë her father was someone very special—and that he'd be proud of her.' And, on a more wistful note, 'I couldn't guarantee that,' she added, 'but at least I hoped it would be true.'

'Oh, Mel…' One swift stride brought him to her again, his arms going round her. 'Why didn't you let me know?' Beneath her hands, his shoulders were like twin rocks. Strong, sturdy, immovable. She laid her head against one.

'I wasn't in any fit state,' she murmured, wishing she could believe that that raw edge to his voice wasn't just because of finding out he had a daughter. 'My mother died two weeks after Kelly.'

'What?' He drew back, looking down into her anguished face, his expression disbelieving, horrified.

'It made all the papers. The story was too new not to.'

'I didn't realise. No one told me. I was in Australia.' He sounded as though he should have known.

'After she died, my own father materialised from out of the blue and insisted I went and stayed with him. I was like an automaton. I could only do whatever he suggested,' she continued, reliving the misery of that time. 'So I stayed with him for a few weeks until I found out all he wanted was the proceeds of the house. It didn't work out anyway, and as soon as I could I moved out. My mother had willed the house to Kelly and me. I gave him some of the money and got myself a small flat with the rest. He would have gambled it all away anyway. I think he went abroad because I never saw him again. But at least I was able to provide some sort of home for my child.'

'Our child,' Vann corrected, his regard hard and analytical. 'Yet you would still have kept it from me. Why, Mel? After how intimate we've been together, you still didn't want me to know.'

'I don't know,' she uttered quickly, avoiding his eyes, because she couldn't tell him. She wasn't sure she even knew herself. 'Anyway, what would you have done? If I'd written and told you I was going to have your baby?'

'Then?' He lifted his head, staring over her shoulder as though at some point in the past. 'What do you think?' he said, his attention returning to her. 'As I told you before—I believe a child should have two parents.'

So he would have honoured his commitments. Married her and provided a home for their baby even though he didn't love her. She wasn't sure whether she could have borne that.

'And what if I'd objected?'

'Then I would have thought it a fitting punishment to drag

you screaming to the altar. The child would have come first.'

Of course. Family ties would mean everything to him because of his childhood, because of how resented he had been made to feel by his own parents.

'And now?' Mel ventured tentatively.

'I want to get to know my daughter,' he asserted, suddenly releasing her. 'Which means that when you go home I want her to stay on here until the school holidays end.'

'No!' A hot emotion seized her, jealously possessive. Still, she should have expected it, she thought. They had come a long way in fourteen years. They had both matured, particularly her, because she had needed to, emotionally at any rate. No longer a lonely adolescent, frightened for the future, she was her own person, independent, successful, her baby nearly a woman. He need make no commitment now to the mother of his child.

'Yes, Melissa,' he countered in response to her firm denial. He only called her that, she realised distractedly, when he was angry with her—or making love... 'You're going to grant me some share in my child's life and give Zoë the chance of a father—a little late in the day but, as I'm sure you'll agree, better late than never—and you'll start by telling her exactly who I am.'

'No!' She could feel the fear like a dark chasm opening up before her.

'If you don't,' he threatened, those strong features grim, uncompromising, 'then I will.'

'All right.' She put up her hands as though to stave off something abhorrent, her eyes tormented, appealing to him. 'But you've got to let me do it my way. In my own time.'

The phone shrilling loudly in the sitting room almost made her jump, her gaze following his towards the sound echoing through the empty villa.

'The time is now, Melissa,' he told her, striding away.

CHAPTER NINE

'WHY didn't you ever *tell* me?' Zoë remonstrated with oh, so Vann-like censure after Mel had told her everything, holding nothing back, later that afternoon. 'Why didn't you let me *know*?'

First there had been shocked disbelief from the teenager, then tears of joy—excitement—and now this rebuke.

'There was only ever that one meeting,' Mel tried explaining gently. 'I didn't think he'd want to know—that he'd want to see us.' And I didn't want you to know what it was like to be rejected, she thought achingly, wanting only to protect her daughter from anything that threatened her happiness—the rejection by her own father and then her stepfather still having the power to hurt.

'You should have told me,' the girl berated her. They were walking in the garden, having picked peppers and courgettes for Marco. From some distance away, behind a pergola of sweet scented jasmine, came the occasional scrape of his hoe on the baked earth. 'Did you love him?'

'Zoë, I was eighteen!' Mel emphasised, uncertain how to answer. 'Just a few years older than you are now.'

'But you must have loved him to have gone to bed with him.' Coming from a twelve-year-old, this was disconcerting, to say the least.

'Yes, I loved him.' Mel sighed. After all, it was true, wasn't it?

'Do you love him now?'

Mel held her breath, unable to meet those enquiring blue eyes beneath the thickly shaped brows. 'It was a long time ago,' she murmured. 'People change.'

'But when you fall in love with someone, I thought it was supposed to be for keeps,' Zoë retorted, kicking at the sandy path with one petulant, sandalled foot. 'That's what you always keep telling me.'

'Not exactly,' Mel countered, deciding her daughter was mixing up romantic love with her views on marriage and commitment. 'It's nice if it can be, but life isn't always like that. Besides, it has to be two-way.'

A frown wrinkled the young forehead. 'You're going out with him,' she stated after some consideration. 'And he's letting us stay here. I thought…'

Dear Zoë. She couldn't yet comprehend the complexities of adult relationships.

'We're just his guests, Zoë. Don't put any more significance on it than that.'

'But he's bound to like you more than any of his last girlfriends.' It was an innocent enough statement, but it sent a shaft of pain spearing through Mel.

'Why?'

'Because of me.'

Putting an arm around the small, bony shoulders, Mel couldn't help giving a cynical chuckle at her daughter's naïvety. If only it were that simple, she thought.

'He said he wants to get to know you. He's asked me to let you stay…' it took an immense effort on Mel's part to put it into words '…after I've gone.'

'What?' Zoë's face lit up. 'Just me on my own?'

Mel wished she could share her daughter's delight, feel great about the fact that her daughter had finally found her father. And she did. Of course she did. But she couldn't help this gnawing anxiety.

'He suggested you stay until the end of the holidays, but I want you home before that.'

'Why?' Zoë asked, pulling away from Mel. She looked defiant, rebellious.

Why? Mel thought quickly. 'Because you have to prepare for school.'

'Ugh! That will take a day! You just want me to go home early because *you* have to,' the girl accused unfairly. 'He's my father and if he wants me to stay longer, I'm staying,' she delivered with her arms folded, an obstinate pout to her mouth.

'And I'm still your legal guardian,' Mel emphasised strongly, wishing she could have avoided this set-to with her daughter. Already she could feel the division, the threat... 'And when I say you're coming home, you're coming home.'

In fact, in the end, what Mel wanted didn't come into the equation. Vann stayed firm, with Zoë only too willing to back him up, so that Mel was left with no choice but to give in.

'Is that child of yours still in Italy?' Jonathan enquired one morning towards the end of August, coming into Mel's office as she was watering a plant on top of her filing cabinet. Though he hadn't actually asked, he seemed to think Zoë was still with Karen, and Mel hadn't been able to bring herself to enlighten him. Nor had she told him, since the need hadn't arisen, that she had spent her second week in Italy at Vann's villa.

'Yes, she's still there,' she responded, relieved to be able to tag on, 'but she's flying home tomorrow.' She was meeting Zoë at the airport around lunchtime and was counting every second. It was the first time Zoë had ever spent a birthday away from her and Mel had missed her unbelievably—not just on her birthday, but over the whole lonely month.

'In that case, why don't we both go out and celebrate tonight?'

'Celebrate?' Mel echoed, eyeing him curiously. He in

turn was eyeing the cheese and tomato sandwich lying, half-eaten, on a paper napkin on her desk.

'I see you're lunching early today.' He grinned, making a great show of consulting his wrist-watch, glinting gold against the golden hairs. It was only ten-forty and he knew she would already have had a light breakfast. 'Must be one of your hungry days. It's just as well then that I've got somewhere special lined up for dinner.'

'Have you?' The thought of Zoë coming home lent added warmth to her smile. 'And what are we celebrating?' she enquired brightly.

'Winning Vann over on to our side. We had the go-ahead to handle all Heywood's new advertising today.' Admiring grey eyes ran over the dark tailored jacket and skirt she wore so well. 'I know we had a few cross words while we were in Italy, but I understand perfectly how a guy like that could turn any woman's head.' Did he? 'After all, I did practically throw the two of you together.' He looked spruce in his dark grey suit, blue shirt and grey and blue striped tie as he placed a file down on her desk. He seemed happy, friendlier towards her, too, than since before the conference. She realised it was because he thought Vann was out of the picture again. 'I'd just like to say, good work, Mel.'

She tried not to let any feelings show beyond those of a professional nature as calmly she accepted the news of the Heywood contract along with Jonathan's praise and his invitation to dinner.

Well, why shouldn't she accept? she thought, after he had gone. Staying in at night, thinking about Vann, was only a recipe for disaster, and that was what she had been doing most evenings since she had come back.

During those last few days in Italy he had been courtesy—even kindness—itself, throwing himself into his new found role of fatherhood with a joy and enthusiasm that had been no less than genuine. One evening he had taken them both to a concert in Ravello, a village situated way up on the rocky mountainside, where they had listened to classical music in the roof-garden of a Norman-Arabian villa.

They had spent hours on his yacht, when he had shown both Zoë and Mel the basics of sailing. Another day they had taken a picnic to a private beach and thrown pebbles into the sea, seeing who could throw the farthest, like a normal, everyday family doing normal, everyday things together. But the uninhibited lover of the previous week had stayed well and truly in the wings, held by a rigid self-discipline that had both frustrated and tortured Mel.

Whether he had wanted to or not, he hadn't touched her, or allowed himself even to be alone with her for any length of time, as if he'd feared that, in doing so, he might be stretching that iron-hard restraint too far. And when the day had come for her to leave, he had let her, driving her to the airport, alone, since Zoë had chosen to stay and help Marco and Quintina harvest the olives. Their conversation had been non-committal on the journey to Naples, their relationship too tenuous to risk anything else. It was when it had been time for her to go through into the departure lounge, before she had even realised what was happening, that he had swept her into his arms, kissing her with a hard finality that had only assured her of what she already knew. That this was goodbye. His breathing had been laboured when he'd released her, as though he had put all his pent-up frustrations over the past week into that one kiss. So why had he been so determined to deny them both?

Tearing into the rest of her sandwich with wounded aggression, Mel forced herself to carry on working, as though she didn't feel this great gaping emptiness inside.

She was the same self-reliant, self-assured woman she had been before she had gone to Positano, she told herself firmly, but knew she couldn't fool herself, even if she managed to fool the rest of the world. Seeing Vann Capella again had changed her.

She didn't feel like going out with Jonathan that evening and it took every ounce of will-power she possessed to get herself ready.

She was in her bathrobe, make-up fixed, hair still loosely swept up from her shower, when the doorbell rang at seven.

Darn it! she thought, wondering why he had to be so early, but when she opened the front door it was with a cry of surprised pleasure.

'Zoë! What are you—?' The girl's arms were around her, her thin jacket wet from the rain that had started as Mel was driving home from work. But it was to the familiar figure of the man standing behind her daughter that Mel's disbelieving eyes flew. 'Vann!'

'Hello, Mel,' he greeted simply, a warm curve to his mouth as he followed the teenager inside.

'What—what are you doing here?' she found she was stammering as Zoë released her, heading straight for the kitchen as she always did, leaving Mel staring up into those formidably attractive features.

'I had to come to London,' he said. 'You didn't think I'd let our daughter come back on her own, did you? It just meant her coming home a day earlier than expected, that's all. I take it that's all right.'

She couldn't remember him closing the front door, but he had. Inside her home for the first time, he was looking curiously past her, along the wide and tastefully decorated hall with its high Victorian ceiling and silk paintwork, to the small mahogany table and her figurine lamp which was casting a pink glow over the walls.

'Yes,' Mel breathed, not thinking straight, because to have him actually standing there in her hallway filled her with an acute longing to throw herself into his arms, bury her face against his broad chest and sob out how much she had missed him. And because even though there were raindrops glistening on his loose hair and dark splashes on his light, casual jacket, the dreary English weather couldn't detract from his tanned magnificence. It was there in the hard vitality of his face, in the dark strength of his throat above the open-necked white shirt he was wearing with light, fitted trousers, so that he seemed almost to have brought a little piece of Italy with him.

'You look beautiful,' he whispered.

So do you, Mel thought, entranced, shaken out of it only by the disappointed young voice calling from the kitchen, 'Mum! There's nothing in the fridge!'

Those steel-hard eyes were watching her solicitously. 'Have you not been eating properly, Mel?'

'In the cupboard!' she shot back over her shoulder. It was where she kept a stock of Zoë's favourite cereal bars. 'I was planning to go shopping tomorrow, on the way back from the airport,' she explained, turning back to Vann. 'I had breakfast, elevenses and lunch. And someone brought in cakes this afternoon.' What did he imagine, that she was pining for him? 'Anyway, I'm going ou—'

She broke off abruptly. Jonathan!

'Yes?' Vann prompted meaningfully.

A cupboard door banged closed, followed by the impatient rustling of paper wrapping.

'I was going out to dinner,' she enlightened him, aware of that shrewd regard on her lightly made-up green eyes, on her smooth complexion, flawless even without the foundation cream she had only just finished applying. Now there was no question of doing anything else but cancelling her arrangements. She couldn't—wouldn't—dream of going anywhere –now that Zoë was home.

'A date?' Vann was behind her as she crossed over to the telephone on the table.

'It's mainly business,' she said.

'Not the obsequious Harvey!'

'He's not obsequious!' Mel snapped, swinging to face Vann, her stomach doing a triple somersault just from looking up into those dark, brooding features. Jonathan might come over as the far too dedicated company man, but that didn't mean she was going to stand for insults on his behalf which, after all, reflected badly on her.

'So it is him!'

God! Why was he always so smug?

'Yes, it's Jonathan,' she took some degree of satisfaction from saying. 'If you must know, he's coming round at seven-thirty.'

'Then you're obviously going to have to put him off,' he advised, a grim determination belying the silky tones. 'And, as you've nothing in the cupboard to feed either yourself or your daughter, you're both going to have to have dinner with me.'

'I can't...' Mel started to protest. Spending any time in his company now, loving him as she did, when it was all so pointless would tear her into little pieces, she thought, before another petulant groan came from the kitchen.

'Mum, is this all there is? I'm starving!'

Lifting the receiver from its cradle, Vann handed it to her. 'Better phone him, Mel,' he said.

Jonathan didn't take very kindly to Vann turning up and ruining his evening. He was already on his way to pick Mel up when he answered his phone.

'What do you mean? Capella's turned up with Zoë? I don't get it. I thought she wasn't coming back until tomorrow. And what's Vann got to do with it?' A car horn blared. It sounded as though Jonathan had just driven into a tunnel.

'I don't want to talk about it now,' Mel responded. She didn't want to talk at all with Vann standing there, coolly watching her. She also didn't think it was a particularly good idea to break the news about Vann and her daughter to Jonathan while he was on the road.

'You've just called off our date and I want to know why and I want to know now!' the MD's voice persisted from somewhere in the dusky suburbs.

Mel's mouth compressed, her eyes making a very expressive attempt at moving Vann into the sitting room. Fortunately, he took heed of her need for privacy and left her to it.

'I thought it was over between you and that guy,' Jonathan pursued as she watched Vann's dominating figure disappearing down the hall. His shoulders seemed to fill the doorway into her sitting room. 'I thought it was just something you had going in Italy. Don't lead him on, Mel. You don't stand a chance of pinning down a guy like that. So why are you letting yourself get so involved with him? And Zoë?'

You asked for it, Mel thought, turning her back on the now empty hall to say simply, 'He's her father, Jonathan.'

'What?' An invective came down the line as though Jonathan had had to make some sudden, swift manoeuvre. Another horn blared. 'You could have told me,' he grumbled after she had answered his further shocked questions with succinct openness.

'I just did,' she snapped, rather unfairly, she thought after she had put down the phone. Jonathan deserved better than that. But she was too keyed up by Vann's unexpected arrival to be her amiable best, especially when he could hear every word she was saying and might try to make something of her conversation with the other man. She could hear him talking to Zoë who had obviously joined him in the living room. They sounded relaxed, intimate, clearly at ease with one another.

'Disappointed, was he?' Vann said dryly when Mel joined him. He was sitting comfortably, long legs crossed at the

ankles, one arm flung carelessly across the back of her settee.

'Not unduly,' she lied, glad that Zoë had gone through
into her bedroom. 'We had a few things to discuss, but they
can wait.'

'I'll bet they can.' He still looked grim but she ignored
his innuendo that there was more to her relationship with
her boss than there actually was.

Let him think so if he wanted to, she thought through a
crushing desire to tell him that Jonathan meant nothing to
her, that there was only one man who had ever made her
feel a complete woman and that was him. But she kept silent
on that score, graciously giving in to Vann's insistence on
taking her and Zoë to dinner, although when it came to
paying the bill in the small Greek restaurant where he had
taken them Mel tried to insist on an equal contribution.

'Scared that letting me pay the bill will constitute surrendering your independence, Mel?' he enquired almost deri-
sively, glancing after Zoë who was heading in the direction
of the Ladies. 'This isn't one of your PR dinners. And tonight I'm not one of your clients. This is called sharing a
pleasant evening with my daughter and the mother of my
child. You denied me any right to do anything for her all
the time she was growing up. Don't deny me this.'

She would have protested further, but something in his
tone tugged at her heart, making her accept his generosity
without any further fuss.

He stayed four days in all, booking into the West End
hotel where he was negotiating a deal with some Japanese
clients.

'Why isn't he staying with us?' Zoë enquired, getting up
the morning after Vann had brought her back, only to find
her father had left shortly after she had gone to bed.

'Because he has to be near the people he's involved with,'
Mel answered, unable to tell her daughter the truth. That

she hadn't invited him to, especially since he had shown no inclination to stay.

Apart from when she had left Naples that day when he had sent her off with that devastating parting kiss, he had shown her nothing but that same cool restraint. All he saw fit to bestow upon her on leaving each evening was a light peck on the cheek, as though his fierce passion for her had burned itself out in the heat of the Neapolitan sun. The only thing binding them together now was Zoë, she accepted painfully, with whom he spent every available moment when he wasn't working.

The evenings, though, were bitter-sweet for Mel. Whether they went out or stayed in, when she cooked dinner for the three of them, as she insisted on doing that last evening of Vann's visit, neither their fascinating discussions on books, music or current affairs after Zoë had gone to bed, nor even their shared humour, could break through the impenetrable barrier that seemed to have sprung up between them.

For Mel it was a strain, and sometimes, particularly during that last evening, she noticed the tense lines about his face and realised that he was finding it a strain, too. Obviously, any sexual involvement with her now that he knew she wasn't just a willing female but the mother of his child, could cause complications he definitely didn't want. Being with her, therefore, had to be taxing his red-blooded urges to the limit, just as being with him and remembering the shameless passion they had shared, was taxing hers. She was only glad that at least Zoë was happy. After all, she tried convincing herself, that was really all that mattered.

The following day was the start of the new school term and Mel would normally have driven Zoë to school on her first morning. But, waking with one of her blinding headaches, Mel was only able to phone for a taxi for the teenager before taking a couple of pain-killers and going straight back to bed.

The doorbell woke her, ringing persistently through the flat.

Her headache was gone, leaving only the usual grogginess, Mel was relieved to discover as she padded, barefoot, down the hallway to the front door.

'Vann!'

'Are you all right?' he asked, his concerned eyes straying briefly down over her short white cotton robe. 'I rang your office. Hannah told me you were off sick.'

She nodded, pulling the door wider to admit him. What was he doing here? Wasn't he supposed to be flying somewhere this morning?

'Yes,' she said, explaining, but not that she had been awake all night wondering how he could leave her with only the usual emotionless kiss, without making any plans to see her again.

It was only then that she realised how awful she must look with no make-up on and her hair falling wildly about her shoulders.

'You've never looked sexier.' He grinned, aware of why her hand had suddenly flown to her face, while her heart seemed to clamour.

In an immaculate dark suit and white shirt, this was one rare occasion when he was sporting a tie, an image which, from his constrained black hair to his gleaming black shoes, was no less than awesome.

With a composure she was far from feeling, she asked, 'Why did you ring the office?'

'I wanted to talk to you. Alone. There are things we need to discuss.'

'Like what?' she queried.

'I don't suppose you've seen this?'

He was unfolding one of the more gossipy tabloid newspapers. It had been folded over at a certain page. There, taken in the busy restaurant where she had met Vann and

Zoë during her lunch-break two days before, was a picture of Mel looking besotted by the dark man sitting across the table from her. Inset, there was a separate picture of Zoë.

'That man with the camera!' she said, aghast. There had been a hen-party or something going on behind them, and she had thought he had been photographing that.

Quickly, Mel took the newspaper from him and read the short article beneath the picture with growing disbelief.

It was all there. Who *she* was. The double tragedy fourteen years ago. Speculation about Zoë. It left nothing to the imagination but that Vann had fathered the child.

'I don't believe this!' Mel breathed, utterly dismayed. Someone had done their homework on her and done it well. 'Why would anyone have wanted to have done this?' she agonised, and knew the answer even before Vann replied.

'Sensationalism. That's all it is. It'll simmer down when there's something more newsworthy to print.'

'Simmer down!' Mel breathed, flabbergasted. 'And what about Zoë? It's her first day back at school. She'll suffer agonies over this when her peers find out.'

'I don't think so,' he said, calmly removing the newspaper from Mel's trembling fingers. 'Unlike you, she hasn't wanted to keep it hidden that I'm her father. She's been telling practically everybody we've bumped into—here and in Italy—so it's hardly surprising someone got hold of the story. Unlike you, my sweet, she seems very proud of the fact.' His tone wasn't very gentle, neither was his endearment. 'I suppose it was bound to become public sooner or later.'

'But it makes it seem as though I...I went to bed with you even though Kelly died. Regardless...' She was shaking her head, unable to bear it. Now everyone would read her shaming secret. Colour suffused her cheeks just thinking about it.

'The truth is, Mel...' the paper rustled as he folded it

again, tossed it down on to her little mahogany table '...you did.'

That wry comment didn't help to make her feel any better. It was all right for him, she thought waspishly. He was used to publicity!

'It wasn't quite like that, and you know it,' she tossed back in defence of her actions. 'But no one's going to know that. People are going to think—'

'To hell with what people think!'

She flinched from his raw anger. 'People believe what they read,' she told him abrasively.

'Yes,' he accepted after a moment, and she wondered if it was remembering how she had been so ready to—and about him—that made his lips compress, made him drag in his breath as though for steadying air.

'I think we should get married,' he said.

'What?' She looked at him incredulously, not sure she had heard him correctly. And when he repeated the statement, 'Why?' she challenged, her heart beating like a bat's wings in her ears. 'Because of that article?'

'Don't be ridiculous,' he said. 'My skin's thick enough to be able to withstand journalistic dross like that. I was going to suggest it even before I saw that paper.'

Was he? She was going weak at the knees.

'Why then?' He couldn't possibly want to, not just for herself, not after the way he could so easily call a halt to any relationship with her even if, for some reason, he was changing his mind about it now. 'Because of Zoë?'

The battle she was having to keep her emotions reined in made her sound as though she were almost jeering his proposal and, from his hard assessment of her, he thought so, too.

'Isn't that a good enough reason?' he asked, his tone devoid of emotion.

No, I want the man I marry to love me! I want you to

love me! But she merely looked at him askance, hurting as she said bitterly, 'To make it legal and above board?'

A nerve twitched on one side of that clean-shaven jaw. 'I don't give a damn about legality or how things look,' he breathed. 'What I do care about is dragging my daughter backwards and forwards between where you are and wherever I might be, because, believe it or not, I want to spend as much time with her as I can. I missed her childhood, but I'm sure as hell not going to miss out on her adolescence. I'm going to be there for her—whenever she wants me—with or without her mother—but, unless you're prepared to be totally selfish, I'm sure you'll agree that I'm making some sense, and say "yes". The kid needs two parents. Living and working together. At least while she's still growing up. When she's an adult—got a stable life of her own—that's different. You can do what you like. Divorce me if you want to.'

Just like that. He was proposing to her like it was some business deal, Mel thought torturedly. A contract that could be terminated as soon as it had been deemed to have served its use.

For a moment she closed her eyes, trying to blot out the sight and sound and scent of him, that subtle spice he used that, without all his other assets and attributes, was working on her senses to try and lure her into accepting one glorious chance to be with him.

But he hadn't said he loved her. How could he, when he didn't? When his world hadn't been knocked off its axis as hers had been? He was only motivated by the misery of his own childhood. That was what was making him insist on marrying her. But, even for Zoë's sake, she couldn't do what he was suggesting. If she did, she would only end up with a heart torn in more pieces, if it were possible, than it was now.

'But I don't love you.' It was agony to say it, but somehow she managed it, and saw his lashes come down, veil any emotion her declaration might have produced.

'I'm not asking you to,' he said, sounding cold and unperturbed. 'Only that you help me provide a loving, secure home for our daughter. We like each other, don't we? Intellectually, we're well suited. And even you can't dispute that we're pretty darn good in bed.'

She wished he hadn't mentioned that. Just the thought of their wild, uninhibited lovemaking while they had been in Italy was making every erogenous zone work overtime. She had to stay strong.

'It was good. But not that good,' she tossed back crazily in a desperate attempt to stave off the temptation of all he was suggesting.

And knew it was a mistake when he said sardonically, 'No? Then perhaps you need reminding.'

'No, Vann!' As he reached for her, Mel's hands flew up to resist him, and met a wall of steel beneath the impeccable suit. But her own body was his ally, an addict for the pleasure that only this man could give her and, even before he swept her up into his arms, she knew it was already too late.

CHAPTER TEN

SHE had been prepared for brutality, a swift, angry pleasure she would nonetheless have welcomed, heightened by enforced abstinence and their weeks apart.

It was therefore a shock to realise that those masculine energies were still governed by an iron control, held in check even when she made him gasp with the most intimate caress of her mouth, even when she lay there, begging him to love her. He seemed determined to take his time and he did, opening her body to his with the prolonged and torturous rapture of his tenderness.

She cried out his name as he took her, and was sobbing as the shuddering spasms of their mutual orgasm ebbed away.

Without a word, Vann eased himself away from her, got up and went into the adjoining bathroom, turning on the shower. Within minutes he had returned, one of her peach bath towels slung around his hips, as he stood with his gaze raking over her tear-stained cheeks, over her mouth, soft and swollen from his kisses.

'Do I take it then that this is your answer?'

Oh, how could he? Mel thought, wanting to tell him that it was because it had been so wonderful that she was crying. Because it had moved her so much that until he had looked at her in that cold, unsympathetic way she had been all for surrendering her very future to him. But how could she? she thought wretchedly, when the reality was that he didn't love her? When he could make any woman feel as though she had died and gone to heaven, simply by taking her to bed, while he remained unaffected and immune?

'Vann, I...' What could she say? Not the truth. Anything but that. It was humiliating enough his knowing that she couldn't resist him sexually. But if he knew of her emotional vulnerability as well, he would use every ounce of persuasion he had to get her to marry him. And it wouldn't take much... 'I can't. It's much too soon. I can't do it. Even for Zoë,' she added to strengthen her argument. It was easier than saying, I want you and need you, and I would never be able to bear it if you decided to leave me. 'And I've got my career...'

'And nothing in the world should be allowed to stand in the way of that!'

'That isn't fair!'

'Isn't it?' he rasped.

'No!' She was sitting up now, holding the duvet to her nakedness, watching from under her spiky lashes as he shrugged back into his clothes.

'It's not just your career, is it, Mel? The reason you won't consent to marry me. I think it goes much, much deeper than that. You're nursing a grievance and it's going to swallow you up, Mel, unless you come to your senses and do something about it before it ruins your life.'

What did he mean? she wondered, aware of him slipping on his shoes, stuffing the tie he'd been wearing unceremoniously into the pocket of his jacket. Was he saying she still had some grudge against men as he'd come right out and accused her of having that day at the villa? Or was it simply because she'd made a fuss the other day when he'd bought Zoë some shoes? Because he'd resented being told that she was responsible for her daughter's clothes? 'When you've sorted yourself out,' he went on, moving away from the bed before she had a chance to challenge him about it, 'perhaps you'll let me know. *If* that day ever comes.'

With that he walked out of the room and a few moments later she heard the front door close firmly behind him.

*   *   *

The next few weeks passed in a blur of misery for Mel. The only time she saw Vann was during his brief visits to collect or return Zoë, on top of which she couldn't help noticing a gradual change in her daughter.

'She's so uncommunicative these days,' Mel confided to Karen over tea at the Ritz during one of the model's regular shopping trips to London. 'Unless she's talking about Vann,' she appended, piqued. 'She can't wait to spend her weekends with him when he comes to London, but she never tells me anything about what she's been doing. I know I'm probably being silly, but I feel I'm losing her, Karen.'

'She's only doing what all normal teenagers do, Mel,' the brunette told her reassuringly, looking willowy in a dark blue blouse and fluid trousers as she poured tea into two delicately patterned cups. 'As for Vann, he asked you to marry him and you refused, so now he's just getting his own back, probably by trying to show you what you're missing. Reading between the lines, I'd say the man was crazy about you,' she concluded laughingly.

With a sudden quickening of her heart, Mel took the steaming cup her friend handed her, but she wasn't convinced. OK, Karen *was* shrewd, she thought. After all, the woman had shown a distinct lack of surprise the last time they had met up, just after Karen had come back from Switzerland, and Mel had told her about her past relationship with Vann.

'I guessed there was more to it than you were letting on,' the ex-model had amazed her by saying, adding with discomfiting canniness, 'And I think there still is.'

But Karen didn't know Vann, Mel told herself, spreading her second scone with a good dollop of strawberry jam. Or the way his childhood had affected him. No, he just thought she was being selfish for not giving in to his demands to— as he thought—put Zoë first. That was why he was getting his own back, she decided. Not for the romantic reason Karen seemed to think.

The half-term holiday came, and with it Vann to take Zoë off to Italy.

'I don't know why you have to keep her the whole week,' Mel complained, folding clothes into the open suitcase on the teenager's bed while Zoë sorted out her toiletries in the bathroom. 'Don't you think that sometimes it would be nice if she could spend some of her free time with her mother?'

'Have you asked her to?'

'What do you think?' Mel looked accusingly up at him standing there on the other side of the single divan. A collection of posters of Zoë's favourite pop idols filled the wall behind him. 'She'd rather spend her time in Campania.' Her tone was clipped, her actions reflecting it as she tossed a light sweater unceremoniously into the suitcase, concluding, 'Much more fun!'

'You can come, too.'

She looked at him quickly, the cool penetration of his eyes on top of that softly delivered statement making her turn away, flummoxed.

'You know I can't.' She had to work, for one thing. For another, he wasn't getting round her like that!

'You could join us, you know, later in the week.' He had already told her that they would be flying back and spending two or three days in Surrey where he had business to attend to. 'I'm sure we'd both appreciate it if you did.'

She knew she could easily have done as he was suggesting and still get to the office, wondering if he thought he could tempt her with the prospect of being waited on for a few days in one of his usual five-star hotels. Because she was tempted, and not just by that. But even his invitation seemed to bracket him and Zoë together, leaving her, Mel, on the outside, and so, shaking her head, she said, 'It's too unsettling, racing off all over the place when I've got so much paperwork to take care of here,' knowing she was only depriving herself by refusing, but she couldn't help it.

'The offer's still open,' he said.

He meant his offer of marriage.

Mel held her breath, every molecule screaming in defiance of her decision not to give in. Just one word. That was all it would take…

'If I remember correctly,' she said, coming round the bed and having to pass him to reach Zoë's small chest of drawers, 'it wasn't exactly the proposal of the century.' Her voice was shaky, body still trembling from the accidental brush of her arm against his shirt sleeve as she selected the skimpy tops that Zoë wanted to take with her.

'With a woman as obstinate as you, Mel, the hearts and flowers didn't somehow seem appropriate.'

She elbowed her way past him. 'So you thought you'd try and bully me into it instead.'

'Is that what you thought I was doing? Bullying you?'

'Wasn't it?' Back on the other side of the bed, she threw the tops down into the case on top of the sweater. 'No woman likes to be told she's only wanted for her child's sake!'

'Well, of course I didn't just mean that.' He glanced over his shoulder, satisfying himself from the clunk of jars and bottles coming from the bathroom that Zoë was still in there. 'I've never been much good with this sentimental stuff, but supposing I told you that…that I want you to marry me because I want *you*. And not just for Zoë's sake, but for mine as well. Because seeing you and not being able to have you is driving me nigh on insane.'

An answering response pierced Mel's loins as she met his darkly intense features across the bed. Dear Heaven! she wanted to believe him. Unwittingly, her gaze fell to the evidence of his hardening arousal and unconsciously she touched her tongue to her top lip, aching for the driving power of his body.

So that was it. Sex. And he knew just how much she craved it with him, she thought, forcing her reckless, shaming need for him under control, realising with a crushing disenchantment the little game he was playing.

'I think,' she said, fixing him with faltering green eyes, 'that you'd say anything to get your own way. After all...' she shrugged '...what have you got to lose?'

'My self-respect,' he said. 'I'm not going to beg, Mel. It wouldn't matter what I said, would it?' He grabbed the handle of the case she had just thrown closed, swinging it off the bed. 'The truth is, you wouldn't believe me if I wrote it in blood!'

Ten minutes later he pulled out of the communal driveway with an excited Zoë, leaving Mel with the cool touch of his lips still lingering on her cheek and the feeling that it was more than just Zoë's company he was taking from her, and she didn't like it.

Throughout that week she kept herself fully occupied, working late or meeting colleagues for dinner to avoid going home to an empty flat. She even enrolled in a yoga class with Hannah, who didn't stop talking about Jack. Only that week, it became apparent to Mel, he had put Hannah out of her misery by finally overcoming his shyness and asking her out. But nothing, especially the younger girl's starry-eyed chatter, could stop Mel thinking about Vann and the life she could be enjoying with him if only she could let herself go and accept him on his terms. After all, because of her mother's two disastrous marriages she was under no illusion about romantic love. And, if she were honest with herself, wouldn't she really have him on any terms rather than suffer this agony of loneliness she was suffering now? So what was stopping her? she wondered, and couldn't really give herself an answer. And, if that wasn't bad enough, Zoë had scarcely spoken to her since she had been away.

It wasn't like the teenager not to keep constantly in touch. Normally she was on the phone at every available opportunity. But obviously Vann was keeping her so amused she didn't feel the need to keep calling her mother, Mel decided, sitting there in her office on Thursday morning, peeved and unhappy. It was just another example of her daughter growing away from her.

But they would be in Surrey now, she reflected, having spoken to Vann and then Zoë even more briefly after their plane had touched down yesterday morning, and telling herself she could have been with them if she hadn't been so stubborn didn't help. She also knew she could have phoned the teenager herself, but she hadn't wanted to appear like the possessive mother. But out of sight was clearly out of mind! And it was all Vann's influence, she told herself bitterly, with hot tears of resentment burning her eyes. He was responsible for taking everyone she had ever loved away from her. Kelly. Her mother. And now Zoë.

She sniffed back her tears, wiping her nose with the back of her hand like some angry adolescent, remembering feeling this loss—this sense of devastation before—and because of this one man. But it wasn't then. It was now.

Reaching for a tissue in her bag and blowing her nose, she told herself to be sensible, to pull herself together. After all, she wasn't an adolescent, she was a grown woman, she reminded herself, and surely able to handle things without falling apart like this!

But at last she was having to face the truth. Perhaps this was what Vann had meant when he had said her career wasn't her only problem. Perhaps this was the grudge he had referred to, this possessive jealousy and resentment that he had been aware of, even when she hadn't. But was she really allowing this deep, psychological hurt to control her life to such a degree?

Perhaps she was, she thought. But that didn't alter the fact that he was doing his level best to come between her and Zoë. And there was no way he was going to get away with that!

Trying to pull his number out of her fuddled brain, she started as the phone in her handbag suddenly began to ring.

Mel knew, the instant she heard Zoë's voice, that something was wrong.

'It's Dad! He's had an accident! I've sent for an ambulance! Oh, Mum, it's awful! You've got to come!' The teenager's words were punctuated by broken sobs.

Oh, God! Quickly Mel sat forward. Her blood felt as if it were leaving her. 'What sort of an accident? Zoë, answer me!' she demanded fearfully, because the youngster was sobbing too much to respond.

'I'm here,' Zoë said at last. 'He was checking something in the loft after the workmen left. They said…they said everything was safe, but the staircase collapsed! Oh, Mum! He isn't moving or anything!'

Wasn't *moving*… Fingers of ice clutched Mel's heart, her brain trying to assimilate what Zoë meant about him checking the loft. What loft?

'Zoë, where are you?'

Trying to stay calm for her daughter's sake, Mel quickly scribbled down the address Zoë gave her.

'So you…you aren't at a hotel,' she observed uncertainly.

'No, it's Dad's house.'

His *house*?

'Oh, Mum, hurry. Please hurry.'

'Are you all alone?'

She wasn't. A neighbour, it seemed, had called only seconds after the accident had happened, had offered to stay until the ambulance arrived.

'I'm on my way,' Mel said simply, before ringing off.

It was a horrendous journey out of London. The traffic was heavy and Mel's patience would have been strained without the added worry of how she might find Vann as well.

Zoë had said he was unconscious. That he'd fallen goodness knew how many feet. But what if he was terribly injured? What if he died? she thought torturedly, the sign for some roadworks blurring before her eyes from the tears she couldn't contain. She loved him and, if he weren't around, nothing in her life, with the exception of Zoë, would have any meaning. She had to find out how he was. She had to!

Stopping at some temporary traffic lights, unable to wait for a more convenient place to pull in, she dived into her bag on the passenger seat for her phone, only to discover that it wasn't there. It was always there, she thought, dismayed, checking pockets she had already checked, until she remembered. She had come out in such a rush she had left it in the office!

She thought of Jonathan and how put out he had seemed when she had said she had to leave at such short notice, and she guessed it wasn't so much the time off as her rushing out to see Vann that he objected to. He hadn't even asked about Zoë, though he'd been interested enough in the client Hannah had shown in just as Mel was leaving his office.

Vann was right about Jonathan, she thought. His interests were only ever self-motivated, his sincerity superficial. Whereas, though Vann might say what he thought, and not necessarily what one wanted to hear, at least he was always truthful. He made no false pretence. At friendship. At being anything he wasn't. At loving…

For what it was worth, he had asked her to marry him—asked her twice, she thought, pulling away from the lights, and both times, like a fool she had refused, flatly and ungraciously, only to realise too late that she wanted to accept—and on any terms—and that the only thing stopping her had been her own petty jealousies and resentments. Too late because she knew, after their last meeting, that he would never ask her again.

Zoë had said she was at his house, she reflected painfully. But Mel hadn't even known he had a house here in England besides the bachelor penthouse pad he used in town. Had he even told her? She racked her brain, realising he could have said he was staying on Mars for all the interest she had taken last weekend when he'd invited her to join him. She'd been too busy thinking up reasons why she shouldn't. And now…

She had left the city behind for the rural suburbs, hardly noticing the autumn landscape, the cattle in the verdant fields. Hardly noticing that the forest through which she had just driven was splashed with flame and gold, merely aware from Zoë's instructions and the dip of the hill, as the road opened out again, that she was almost there.

Mel steered, braked, changed down the gears and, coming out of the bend, gasped as she caught her first view of Vann's house.

Nestling in its own valley, at the end of a long, descending drive, it was a period, stone-built manor. Large enough for one to be able to breathe, but not so large as to be ostentatious, Mel decided, the adjoining woodlands beyond the rambling gardens and the quiet lake marking it out as a hideaway for the wealthy.

It was with trepidation that she knocked on the front door a few moments later. What would Zoë tell her? she wondered with her stomach muscles knotting. Or would she have gone to the hospital and left the neighbour to break the news?

How she got through the next few moments she wasn't sure, but she thought her legs would buckle in suspense

when the door opened and a relieved-looking Zoë said,
'Mum! I've been trying to ring you! I've been trying and
trying but all I kept getting was voice-mail—'

'Why? What's happened?' She was over the threshold,
her hands fearful, gripping on the girl's slender shoulders.
'Oh, Zoë, how is he? Tell me!'

CHAPTER ELEVEN

'It's all right,' Zoë said. 'Mum! It's all right! That's why I've been trying to reach you. He's—' A sudden movement made the teenager turn, and Mel looked up.

'Vann!'

In blue denim from head to foot, his hair unusually tousled, he looked, as he emerged from one of the rooms off the spacious hall, big and strong and incredibly sexy. Not like an invalid lying injured somewhere. Not dying, as she'd let her imagination convince her he was, but very much alive!

Her throat clogging with emotion, she watched his measured approach, feeling his hard assessment of her grey trouser-suit, her pale and probably, she realised, very blotchy face, but she was too overwhelmed even to care.

'Tears, Mel?' They were welling into her eyes even as he said it. 'Over me? Surely not?'

'I thought…' She stopped, unable to go on and saw his chin lift in the subtlest gesture towards Zoë.

'Oh, well… I'll leave you two guys to it,' the girl announced, as though making up her own mind. 'Dad's bought me this fantastic pop video. It's really, really cool!' She made to run off, but then stopped, hair flying as she pivoted round and, with her young features turning more serious, said, 'I'm glad you came, Mum.' She shot a kind of triumphant look towards her father. 'I'm really glad you're here.'

Through misty eyes, Mel watched her daughter's swift retreat up the wide mahogany staircase. The whole place smelled of new wood, fresh plaster and paint.

She turned back to Vann, her eyes guarded, questioning. 'Zoë said you were injured.'

He was reaching around her. 'Zoë overreacted.' His achingly familiar scent, as he pushed the door closed, seemed to erase all the others. But, glancing over her shoulder, Mel noticed the pain that even that simple action had caused him.

'You *are* hurt!' Without a thought, her hands flew to help him. 'Why aren't you in hospital? Zoë said—'

'I'm all right,' he told her, but didn't resist the tentative arm she put out to assist him through the nearest doorway into the large yet comfortable sitting room, his hand clutching his ribs. 'I—don't need a—hospital.' Wincing between words, he dropped heavily down on to the rich burgundy settee that matched the thick brocade curtains and a large standard lampshade behind one of the easy chairs. 'Zoë just panicked.'

'But she said you were knocked out…'

'I've been knocked out by a lot of things in my time, but I always recover.' Cynicism hardened his voice, the painful twist of his smile.

'Vann, don't,' she whispered.

'Why not? You're not going all sentimental on me, are you? That's not like you at all.'

The pained lines etching his face made him look harder, more formidable than ever and, ignoring the gibe, she glanced away, absently absorbing his impeccable taste in the surrounding décor and furnishings. If she'd had a free hand with this room she might have chosen the same things herself, she appreciated distractedly. That painting over the fireplace. The warm colours. The style of that chair…

'Of course you'll want to take Zoë home.'

She looked at him quickly. 'Why do you say that?'

'Isn't that the main reason you're here?'

'No.' I want to stay and look after you, she nearly said, but checked herself. She didn't want to tell him while he was in this mood. 'She said she'd sent for an ambulance. What did you do? Make her cancel it?'

'You're darn right I did!' he said, ignoring the small reproof in her voice. 'She didn't want to, but I insisted.'

She could see Zoë protesting over the ambulance, imagine the battle of wills that would probably have ensued. But, unlike with her, Mel thought, when sometimes she had to yield to her daughter's intractable spirit, Vann would have got his way.

'I was going to bring her back early tomorrow in any case.' Pain furrowed his brow as he shifted his position slightly. 'Something's come up that means my going away—indefinitely. Or it will, as soon as these infernal bruises heal. I'll send for her sometimes. I don't intend losing touch with my daughter. But you were right. It was wrong of me to try and force you into marrying me—to try and put something there that wasn't. Wrong of me even to pursue you when you so clearly didn't want to get involved. God!' He laughed harshly at the air, wincing from the sudden movement. 'You told me enough times! It was my own fault for being conceited enough to think I could ever change your mind—that you might have changed your mind about me. But you've never really forgiven me, have you, Mel?'

She dropped down on to the settee. 'For what?' she whispered.

And realised, even before he said, 'For your mother— your sister. But I thought you'd had your pound of flesh fourteen years ago—over Kelly, at least. After that note you sent I could only deduce that that was your reason for sleeping with me. I told myself you were young and hurting. That it was understandable if you wanted to lash out at me...'

'Lash out at you? What do you mean?' She couldn't understand what he was saying.

'What else could I take it to mean? After the experience we shared. How close we got. Letting you know I wanted to see you again. Those four little words said it all—really gave me my comeuppance. *Thanks but no thanks*!'

'What are you talking about?' she queried, baffled.

'Your note. The one you wrote to me after our first night together.'

'But I never wrote anything like that,' she breathed. 'I sent you my number like you asked me to—and I said one or two other things, but it wasn't that. I'd never have said that.' How could he have believed that about her?

'Oh, come on, darling. It might have been in the heat of the moment—'

'It wasn't. I *didn't* write it.' Mel's teeth were almost clenched with the effort of trying to convince him. But she had to tell him. She loved him too much for him to go on thinking the worst about her and, steeling herself, she said, 'I'd never been with anyone before—not like that—and I wanted to tell you.' And she had, scribbling it down so joyously on the hotel's headed notepaper, convinced in her girlish innocence that he'd be flattered. 'I only intended to jot down my number, like you asked, but when I started writing I couldn't stop. I told you that it was my first time—that I'd been a virgin—and how what we had done was so special, had meant so much to me. I said how sorry I was about all you'd had to go through in your life and how much I was looking forward to hearing from you again. I thought, when you didn't reply, that I'd scared you off. That I'd sounded like a love-struck kid instead of the experienced type of girl you probably thought I was. But that's what I wrote. Not anything so vindictive and nasty as you're suggesting.'

Something besides incredulity lit the steely blue eyes. 'Then…' His face was lined now with puzzlement rather than pain. 'If it wasn't you, who…?'

'I don't know. I left it for Bern Clayton to give to you when—'

'Clayton.' Contempt was suddenly giving way to a hard, dawning clarity. 'So that's how he...' His sentence tailed off, his voice almost cracking. 'We'd had a row about my wanting to leave—give up the whole music scene. He would have been prepared to do anything to keep me on the road—lining his pockets. That sheet of paper was torn—over half of it missing...' he reflected aloud. 'Just those words under your reminder that I'd asked you to contact me. If you didn't write them, then I suppose he could have doctored your letter—added that vengeful little comment to make me think...to remove any reason for my wanting to stay in England...'

'What do you mean? He substituted what I'd said—and you believed it for all these years? Thought I'd written something so horrible?' she stressed, unable to comprehend herself how anyone could do anything so cruel. And when his eyes narrowed, as though he still couldn't quite come to terms with what she was saying: 'You were the one who told me not to believe everything I read, and you've done just that,' she pointed out. 'Been guilty of the very thing you accused me of in the beginning. For all this time...' Not surprising then that he had thought she had slept with him just to get her own back. To bruise his ego in the most basic way because of what had happened to Kelly. 'No wonder you didn't bother to contact me. And I thought—'

'Oh, but I did.'

'You did?' Her head came up in a blaze of fire. 'When?'

He shrugged. 'Oh, some months later. When I came back from Australia, although I must admit it was a rather half-hearted attempt after what you...what I thought you'd written. After all the publicity over...well, you know... I found the address where Kelly had lived—even contacted it—but there were new people there and no one had heard of Lissa

Ratcliffe. I didn't realise then that Kelly had been your half-sister and that Lissa wasn't even your real name.'

So he had come looking for her. Had wanted to find her again. How different life would have been if he had! she thought with a flash of pain.

'Is that why you tried to keep me at a distance when we met again in Italy? Because you thought I'd ignored your letter?' he asked wonderingly as the truth sank in. 'Do you really think I'd have ignored it if I'd received something from you like that?'

'Wouldn't you?'

'You really believe that?' He swore viciously, all his vehemence directed towards his old manager.

'You're in pain,' she murmured, her eyes anxious, when the sudden effort of moving made him wince again.

'Too hell with that!' He was reaching for her, and warmth and need and excitement ran through her as he sank back against the sofa, dragging her with him across his chest. 'Oh, my poor love.' He was stroking her hair, his hand strong and warm against her temple. 'What must you have thought of me? Don't you know I'm crazy about you? That I've always been crazy about you?'

'Oh, Vann.' She couldn't believe what she was hearing, her senses already spinning from the warm, hard contact of his body. Even injured, she could feel its latent power, and he smelt nice, too, so fantastically masculine.

'I just couldn't seem to find a way to show you. Or to make you see that what we had together wasn't just sex. That it was more than that. On both our parts. Because you do love me, don't you?' One strong hand crushed the wild flame of her hair at the nape of her neck, pulling her head back. 'Don't you?' He spoke with a raw emotion that threatened devastation to himself—and her—if she denied it.

'Yes.'

'Then let me hear you say it.'

'I love you. I love you! I love you!'

He exhaled sharply, burying his face against the perfumed column of her throat. 'Then why have you been so determined to keep us apart?' The pain was there in his voice. Not physical pain this time, but something deep and raw and impassioned.

'I don't know,' she admitted meekly. 'I was afraid.'

He lifted his head, eyes uncomprehending. 'Of what?'

'I don't know.' She tried to think, her expression as tortured as his. 'Lots of things. You didn't ever commit yourself, for one thing.'

'How could I?' His tone was disbelieving. 'You wouldn't ever give me the chance.'

'Only because I thought you only wanted to marry me to make it right for Zoë.'

'Only to—' He sighed heavily, shaking his head. 'I asked you to marry me, quite simply, because I love you, Mel. Surely you must have realised that?'

'But that week at the villa—you didn't want to sleep with me. You didn't even want to touch me!'

He gave an almost derisive chuckle at that. 'Didn't want to sleep with you? Not want to touch you?' He looked staggered that she could think so. 'Do you realise the battle I had keeping my hands to myself every time I looked at you? But I only insisted on separate rooms—tried to keep our relationship so low-key—because I wanted to prove to you that I was serious about more than just your body. I also wanted to prove it to myself because I was so wild for you all the time. I've never met a woman I've wanted so much, and I wanted to be sure it wasn't just some deranged state of infatuation that would fade if it were denied its most fundamental force. And you must admit, darling, it's one hell of a force between us. As for anything else, do you really think I'd marry someone I didn't love—who didn't love me—and make two—no, three—people's lives miserable simply to make things legal? I know I've got some old-fashioned values, but they aren't quite that archaic!'

'But you said I could divorce you as soon as Zoë was grown up…'

Momentarily, a cleft appeared between his brows. But then he laughed for the first time, showing his strong white teeth.

'Oh, you little fool!' he said with a smile. 'That was only because I was at my wits' end over how I was going to get you to marry me. I thought you'd be more inclined to if you felt you weren't making a lifelong commitment—that you wouldn't feel so tied. But that was simply desperate measures for a desperate man.'

'I wouldn't have refused,' Mel admitted then, 'if I'd known how you felt.'

'Do you believe me now?'

For answer she reached up and, slipping a hand behind his head, tilted her lips to meet his. 'You'll just have to keep telling me,' she whispered.

Those arms around her tightened and he said, 'I love you, Mel. With my heart. With my mind. With my body. I think I fell in love with you that first night when you came to my hotel, although I didn't know it then, not until afterwards when I received that terrible note I thought you'd written. But that night you gave me something to believe in. You seemed so lost and yet at the same time so courageous. I'd never met anyone who seemed so totally trusting—so sincere. When we made love, you gave of yourself as though I mattered. As though I were a real human being and not just some craved idol you were acting out a fantasy with.' As must have happened, she thought, with some of the girls he'd been involved with then. 'That's why I wanted to see you again, not only to know you were all right but because I think, even then, I recognised your capacity for loving. I wanted a share in it. I thought I could qualify. That's why it seemed like such a comeuppance to be sent that note.

'When I saw you again, that day at the beach, even though I didn't recognise you, I sensed something so profound between us I knew I had to pursue it, whatever the cost. Afterwards, when I found out about Zoë, I couldn't have been more pleased, but I was angry too because you hadn't told me she was mine. I thought it was because you really didn't like me very much—you seemed so adamant about not getting involved with me. I've tried telling myself that you wouldn't have responded to me in the way you did if you didn't care anything for me—yet...'

From what he left unsaid she recalled her unspeakable behaviour towards him.

'I've just been so scared,' she admitted quietly. 'Scared of making a commitment. Scared of losing Zoë. Oh, Vann! I've been so mixed up.'

'You're telling me, my love,' he murmured indulgently against her ear, cradling her in his arms, his lean hardness evoking those primal feelings in her. She didn't feel insecure any more. 'That's why I came over so heavy-handed at times, because I knew someone had to take charge of your life. For a company director you were making a pretty good hash of it. And I've never wanted to take Zoë away from you—only to share her with you. That's why I bought this place when it came on the market recently. I was hoping that eventually I could make it a home for all of us. Some parts of it were in a bad state of repair—' he grimaced '—the back staircase being one of them. But I've had work done—and not always satisfactorily,' he said, reminding her of how he might have been killed through someone else's negligence, 'for the past few weeks. I knew it wouldn't be too far for you to commute and I wanted so much for you to share it. I wanted to surprise you. I must admit on that score I had a good team. I couldn't have done it without Zoë.'

Mel's glance swept over the room—so pleasing to her taste, her mind going back over the past few weeks to her daughter's secretiveness, her eagerness to be with her father. She had thought the girl just didn't want to be with her. And all the time…

'Just wait until I see her,' she threatened jokingly, her eyes shining with joy. 'And the job be hanged!' Until today, she hadn't realised how little it meant to her. 'I'll go anywhere where you are. To the moon if you want me to. Stay here and make a home for you, if that's what you want.'

He put up his hands, laughed, and said. 'Hey, steady on! Is this Ms Sheraton speaking? No, I wouldn't demand that of you. You wouldn't be happy unless you were out there tackling new innovations. Clinching deals. The only stipulation in this relationship will be that you keep the master's bed warm and give some consideration to letting him make you the mother of all his children.'

'Is that all?' A kick of desire made itself felt deep in her lower body. She wanted him so much. 'A pity we can't start now.' Her hands were already moving inside his shirt.

'You're sure you want that?' He sounded uncertain.

'I'd like nothing better than to have another baby with you, but to watch it grow up together this time. And I know Zoë will be thrilled. Only…'

'Only what?' he queried, seeing her frown.

'You said you were going away.' A little cloud settled on her sunny horizon.

'Only on our honeymoon.'

'But you said…'

'What I said was that something urgent had come up— which it has in one of my European companies—and that I might be going away indefinitely, which I was prepared to do until you came here and I realised how much you cared.

I didn't think I could stay here any longer, needing you so much and thinking I could never have you. I would have kept in constant touch with Zoë, but, my dearest, I just couldn't bear it, thinking I was driving a wedge between you. And another rejection from you would have been too much to take. As it is…'

'As it is?' she queried, catching the sensual note in his voice.

'As it is,' he said, 'I'm quite happy to delegate responsibility to one of my senior management. I think, darling, you'll have to help me upstairs, because something far more pressing has come up here.'

'You're injured!' She laughed, heart leaping from his innuendo. But she could see what he meant.

'I've still got hands, haven't I?' His smile was wicked. 'So have you.' His gaze dropped, assessed, appreciated. 'A beautiful mouth, too. Besides, that pop video's going to last for at least another hour.'

And suddenly she was lying fully across his lap, locked in his arms, any sign of the pain he was suffering lost in his groan of satisfaction as his tongue penetrated the soft mouth that parted so willingly beneath his. 'Mel. My beautiful Lissa. Melissa.' In his whispered words there was sensuality and torture and awe. 'I'm not presuming too much, am I? You really do want to marry me?'

With his hands sliding down her body it was difficult to respond to anything but the raw pleasure of the moment. She was drowning in the rapture of their mutual love and need and desire. But she thought of the years that had been wasted. That cruel note from his rogue of a manager that must have torn him apart—torn both of them apart, until now. And, in response to his proposal, and the sudden thrill of his fingers on her bare midriff sliding upwards again, searching, teasing, creating ecstasy, she murmured, 'Yes, oh, yes. Yes, please…'

Modern Romance™
...seduction and
passion guaranteed

Tender Romance™
...love affairs that
last a lifetime

Medical Romance™
...medical drama
on the pulse

Historical Romance™
...rich, vivid and
passionate

Sensual Romance™
...sassy, sexy and
seductive

Blaze Romance™
...the temperature's
rising

27 new titles every month.

Live the emotion

MILLS & BOON®

MB3

MILLS & BOON®

Live the emotion

Modern Romance™

THE MISTRESS PURCHASE by *Penny Jordan*

Leon Stapinopolous has never known defeat in the
boardroom – or in the bedroom! His acquisition of one
of France's oldest perfume houses is just another notch
in his business profile – but he insists that stunning
perfume designer Sadie Roberts is included in the
purchase price!

THE OUTBACK MARRIAGE RANSOM by *Emma Darcy*

At sixteen, Ric Donato wanted Lara Seymour – but they
were worlds apart. Years later he's a city tycoon, and
now he can have anything he wants… Lara is living a
glamorous life with another man, but Ric is determined
to have her – and he'll do whatever it takes…

A SPANISH MARRIAGE by *Diana Hamilton*

Javier married Zoe purely to protect her from male
predators who were tempted by her money and her
beauty – he has all the money he could ever need. But
as their paper marriage continues he finds it increasingly
hard to resist his wife – even though he made her a
promise…

HIS VIRGIN SECRETARY by *Cathy Williams*

Italian millionaire Bruno Giannella is every woman's
dream. So Katy thinks she must be dreaming when he
demands she become his live-in secretary! But Bruno is
convinced there's a sensual woman hiding beneath Katy's
timid mousy exterior…

On sale 2nd April 2004

*Available at most branches of WHSmith, Tesco, Martins, Borders,
Eason, Sainsbury's and all good paperback bookshops.*

0304/01a

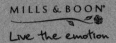

FREE

4 BOOKS
AND A SURPRISE GIFT!

We would like to take this opportunity to thank you for reading this Mills & Boon® book by offering you the chance to take FOUR more specially selected titles from the Modern Romance™ series absolutely FREE! We're also making this offer to introduce you to the benefits of the Reader Service™—

★ FREE home delivery
★ FREE monthly Newsletter
★ FREE gifts and competitions
★ Exclusive Reader Service discount
★ Books available before they're in the shops

Accepting these FREE books and gift places you under no obligation to buy; you may cancel at any time, even after receiving your free shipment. Simply complete your details below and return the entire page to the address below. **You don't even need a stamp!**

YES! Please send me 4 free Modern Romance™ books and a surprise gift. I understand that unless you hear from me, I will receive 6 superb new titles every month for just £2.69 each, postage and packing free. I am under no obligation to purchase any books and may cancel my subscription at any time. The free books and gift will be mine to keep in any case.

P4ZEF

Ms/Mrs/Miss/Mr ....Initials ....
BLOCK CAPITALS PLEASE

Surname ....

Address ....

....

....Postcode ....

Send this whole page to:
UK: FREEPOST CN81, Croydon, CR9 3WZ
EIRE: PO Box 4546, Kilcock, County Kildare (stamp required)

Offer valid in UK and Eire only and not available to current Reader Service subscribers to this series. We reserve the right to refuse an application and applicants must be aged 18 years or over. Only one application per household. Terms and prices subject to change without notice. Offer expires 30th June 2004. As a result of this application, you may receive offers from Harlequin Mills & Boon and other carefully selected companies. If you would prefer not to share in this opportunity please write to The Data Manager at the address above.

Mills & Boon® is a registered trademark owned by Harlequin Mills & Boon Limited.
Modern Romance™ is being used as a trademark.
The Reader Service™ is being used as a trademark.